By ROWENA SUDBURY

NOVELS
The King's Tale
The King's Heart

Blue Moon
Promises and Lies

Published by DREAMSPINNER PRESS
http://www.dreamspinnerpress.com

The King's Heart

ROWENA SUDBURY

Dreamspinner Press

Published by
Dreamspinner Press
382 NE 191st Street #88329
Miami, FL 33179-3899, USA
http://www.dreamspinnerpress.com/

The King's Heart

Cover Art by Anne Cain   annecain.art@gmail.com
Cover Design by Mara McKennen

ISBN: 978-1-61372-545-0

Printed in the United States of America
First Edition
June 2012

eBook edition available
eBook ISBN: 978-1-61372-546-7

My sincere thanks are given to the staff at Dreamspinner Press for their tireless and thorough support. Much thanks to Lynn West for helping me become a better writer and for being so patient. To Mara McKennen for her beautiful covers. Special admiration and thanks to Elizabeth North for taking a chance on me and for being in my corner always.

I would also like to recognize the tireless support and constant encouragement that comes from my friend, Danyel. She gave me the inspiration for *The King's Tale* and has never stopped helping along the way. My toughest critic—and my biggest fan—I am fortunate to call her friend.

My writing would not be possible without the unwavering support of my family. My mom and dad taught me to believe in myself and have always been there for me. They also encouraged my love of history and the finer things in life. My son Peter listens to all my ideas and offers great insights.

The love and support I receive from my husband, Dave, is something that requires more than a simple thank you. Through thick and thin, better and worse, he is always there. I would not understand the true nature of a loving relationship if I did not have him, and for that I will ever be grateful.

Glossary

Anwyll (ah-NOO-il)
Anwylyd (ah-NOO-lid) — beloved/a loved one
Bachgen (BACH-ken) — boy
Beraidd (BER-eith) — sweet
Beunydd (BUE-nith) — daily
Cariad (care-EE-ad) — beloved
Carradoc (care-RAH-doc)
Carys (CARE-iss)
Ci bach ffol (key bach fol) — foolish puppy
Corranyeid (Cor-an-YAY-id)
Dafydd (DAV-ith)
Diawl (DEE-owl) — devil
Dinbych-y-Pysgod (dinn-bick ah PAHS-gahd)
Dwi eiddoch (DWI eye-DOCH) — I'm yours
Edifar (eh-DI-var) — sorry
Eiddoch/Eiddof (EYE-thoc/EYE-thov) — mine
Fy llew (vy LOO) — my lion
Glamorgan (Gla-MOR-gan)
Gwnei 'm balfalu da (GWYN-eye EM bal-VAL-i DA)
    — You make me feel good
Llanilltud Fawr (Lan-ILL-tid VOW-er)
Llevelys (Hlev-EL-iss)
Llew ffyrnig (loo FEER-nig) — fierce lion
Lludd (HLEETHE)
Llwglyd (LOO-glid) — hungry
Lysnowydh (Li-SNOW-ith)
Nef (NEV) — heaven
Ond eiddo (OND EYE-tho) — I belong to you
Prydferth (PRID-verth) — beautiful
'Rwy'n dy garu di (ROO-een dee GAR-ry dee) — I love you
Strasnedh (STRAHS-neth)

❦ 1 ❦
Lysnowydh

THE kingdom of Lysnowydh was perched upon a high cliff overlooking the wild Cornish coast, far enough away from London to dodge the intrigues of King Henry III's court. The Earl of Leicester raged against King Henry that he but peopled his court with unsavory Frenchmen, relations of the Queen Consort Eleanor. In the main it did not trouble Lysnowydh's King Christopher, nor did he feel compelled to enmesh himself in their struggles. Christopher's own kingdom had endured enough strife and hardship, and once these hardships were settled he was content to remain in his own corner of the world.

Lysnowydh was thrust upon Christopher after the untimely death of his father. It rankled, as he felt as though he was not through sowing his wild oats, yet he settled down and assumed the yoke of kingship. Early on, his council pressed for him to find a suitable mate and provide an heir for the kingdom, lest it be overrun by the nefarious king of Strasnedh, Warin. Christopher refused to settle for anything less than love, and when he found love within the cottage of Dafydd, formerly the kingdom's woodsman, there was much dissension from his council, since such a union would not provide the needed heir. In defiance, and with love in his heart, Christopher took Dafydd as his handfasted mate, with permission granted by King Henry. Soon after, he took Lady Marged into his household, and although he and Dafydd were newly joined, he began to split his time between them as he strove to get Marged with child.

Treacherous and full of dark yearning, King Warin designed a plan to bring Christopher's idyll crashing down. He abducted Marged from beneath Christopher's nose and arranged a trade between her and Dafydd. Torn to the very core, Christopher was forced to comply, returning to Lysnowydh with his unborn heir while leaving his handfasted mate in the evil king's clutches. By virtue of siege and trickery, Christopher rescued Dafydd, and Strasnedh was very nearly destroyed in the process. Although Dafydd recovered, a shadow of the torture visited upon him still cloaked his every move. Angry at the injustices visited upon Lysnowydh by Warin, King Henry banished him under threat of excommunication. Strasnedh was ceded to King Christopher.

Once the heir, Anwyll, was born, Christopher gave leave for marriage between Marged and one of his most trusted knights, Sir Patrick. Strasnedh was held in stead by Sir Patrick, as it was Christopher's wish that one day it be given to Anwyll.

Now, as the warmth of summer gave way to the chill of fall, all gathered within the hall at Lysnowydh for the main meal at day's end. As was the custom, Dafydd sat at Christopher's left hand to share his plate. Marged and Patrick were given seats of honor on the dais, and the lesser nobles occupied the trestle tables below. Once Father Geoffrey gave the blessing and pages came forward with bowls for hand washing, the meal was served. Christopher watched as ruby-red wine was poured into his goblet, and then he took it up and sprawled back in his chair.

"'Tis well," he said after he had drunk deeply. "The cattle are fat, the wheat sleepy in the warm sun. Our future looks bright indeed."

"Aye," said Dafydd as he deftly speared the choicest slices of rare beef from the serving platter and laid them on Christopher's trencher. "Ere long 'twill be winter."

Christopher took up a slice of beef on his knife and winked as he popped it in his mouth. "Winter brings long nights under warm furs."

"You are wicked, my king," Dafydd murmured.

"'Tis truth," Christopher said, "and well you know it. In any case, 'tis my experience that reward comes to those who are wicked."

"Betimes aye," Dafydd said absently.

Below the table Christopher rested his hand on Dafydd's thigh for the briefest moment, thus communicating his support and understanding. He leaned forward and whispered into Dafydd's ear, "Wicked for sexual gain is not the same as wicked for wicked's sake." He squeezed and then released Dafydd's leg. "I trust this night you would reward me for the former."

"Aye," came Dafydd's soft reply. "Mayhap."

"Now who is wicked?" Christopher said with a chuckle as he leaned back in his chair.

"Ah, your majesty," Dafydd said pointedly, "I have learned from one who is the master of the game."

Color flamed across Christopher's cheeks, and he turned and presented Dafydd his back. A shiver of anticipation coursed through Dafydd's body at the prospect of the night to come. As he continued his meal, he listened with half an ear as Christopher took up conversation with Patrick and Marged.

"It has been six months and more since last we checked on Strasnedh. Enough time has passed. We must needs take a contingent forth, see the lay of the land and whether the keep can be refurbished, or if it must needs be razed and begun afresh."

"Aye, your majesty," Patrick said, and he bowed his head. "'Tis not my intent to make free with your generous offer to house us here forever."

"Nonsense," Christopher said, his voice louder than he had intended. He swallowed and continued in a more modulated tone. "'Tis my desire to give you shelter, you and Marged and my son Anwyll, for as long as is needed. Strasnedh must be made habitable before I will toss any of you out into the cold of coming winter."

"Peace, your majesty," Patrick said. "'Twas not my intent to anger you, 'tis just that...."

"'Tis just what?" Christopher paused in his eating to hear what Patrick had to say.

By his side, Dafydd also paused and laid his knife upon the table.

Patrick bit his lip and reached for Marged's hand. He spared one glance at Dafydd and then said softly, "We must needs call for Sir Richard ere we venture forth to Strasnedh. 'Tis my belief—" and here he faltered.

Understanding began to dawn, and Christopher urged Patrick to continue. "Go on, young Patrick."

"I do not believe Sir Dafydd wishes to join us when we go."

"Ah," Christopher said. "I had not meant that he join us." He turned, cast a quick look in Dafydd's direction, and then turned back to face Patrick. "Yet you have the right of it. We must needs send for Sir Richard." He took up his knife again. "Monday next, we shall set up. Speak with Sir Walter; have the message sent first thing on the morrow."

"Aye, your majesty. 'Twill be as you wish."

Talk then turned to lighter subjects, and when the meal was through, Christopher rose from the table and beckoned Dafydd to follow him above stairs. On the landing Christopher continued into his room to have his body servant Alain help him undress, Dafydd went into his own room alone.

Most nights found Christopher and Dafydd sharing the bed in Dafydd's chamber. While it was smaller than Christopher's, it was not lacking in richness of appointment. Although it was late summer outside, the interior of the castle was cool, and furs covered the bed. Dafydd deigned to have his manservant help him disrobe, and on this night he waited naked in the bed. Soon enough Christopher appeared through the connecting door from his own room, clad in a bed robe that he dropped before he climbed up to join Dafydd.

"Shhh," Christopher crooned as he placed his finger over Dafydd's lips. "No talk of Strasnedh this night." His finger was a gentle caress on Dafydd's lips, and he tipped his head to the side. "I would have you reward me for my wickedness."

Dafydd opened his mouth, took Christopher's finger inside, sucked down to the knuckle, and then drew back to the tip. "I had no wish to speak of aught which would damp our love this night, my king."

"Ahh," Christopher said, and he moved closer, cupped a hand around the small of Dafydd's back. "And yet I saw questions in your eyes."

"Hush," Dafydd murmured. "I would taste you this night, free from Strasnedh's shadow."

"Are you hungry, cariad?" Christopher asked.

"Aye, my hunger for you is always great."

Christopher moved back and peeled away the furs from their bodies. "Then you must needs sup, lest you wither away to nothing." He turned and settled back on the bed against the smooth sheet.

Candles bathed them in golden light. Dafydd loomed up above, drank in the sight of Christopher's glowing body, and cast his gaze upward from the stirring erection, over softly rounded belly, up over rosy cheeks. It was not often that Christopher was this quiescent; it was his wont to be the devouring lion.

"You enflame me with your eyes," Christopher murmured, "but 'tis your mouth I would have."

"Are you impatient?" Dafydd asked. He passed his tongue over his lips, still lingering on his knees above the king.

"Scoundrel!" Christopher reached up and wound his fingers through Dafydd's short hair, pulled him down closer. He arched his back as Dafydd's mouth closed over his length, and released his hair as he braced his heels against the covers.

Dafydd reached up to tuck his hands under Christopher's hips. He opened his eyes once to see the pleasure etched upon the king's face and then gave way to the gratification he always derived from pleasuring Christopher this way, the scent deep in his nostrils, the velvety taste of hardened flesh. Something tickled at the back of his mind, warning that it wouldn't last as long as he wanted it to; it never did. Vaguely he wondered if Christopher would ever allow him to tie his hands that he might tease him to the brink more than one time before sending him over the edge.

Upon the heels of that thought, Christopher surged from the bed and neatly reversed their positions. With a strong hand, he held Dafydd against the covers and reached with the other for a fingerful of cream from the ready pot at the bedside.

"'Tis always the same, cariad," Christopher growled while his fingers found their mark. "I wonder, will the day ever come that I tire of this?"

"You will not—" and the last word was torn from Dafydd's lips as Christopher slammed inside him. Dafydd's hands curled in the cast-aside furs as he was swept away in Christopher's fierce taking.

What was left unsaid between them fueled their coupling. Enough time had gone by that this roughness did not hurt Dafydd, yet it still weighed heavily on both of their souls. In the magic times when daily drudgery was left aside, their shared, cloudy past was outshone by the sunshine of their love. And when they found release together, as they did this night, it was all but forgotten.

The candlelight wavered, sending long shadows over the interior of the bed hangings. Christopher lazed against Dafydd's side.

"You must needs douse the candle and stoke the fire, cariad. You have sapped my strength."

Dafydd grunted, "Not yet awhile." He turned to nuzzle along the top of Christopher's head. "I would be greedy, soak this in."

"As always, you are a poet, and yet I am feeling indulgent."

"'Tis well."

2

Changes Wrought

WHEN the week had passed, Sir Richard arrived in Lysnowydh. Ever mindful of Dafydd's soft soul, he did not press him to join them in the journey to Strasnedh. As it was, he saw the pain shadowing Dafydd's eyes whenever the subject of Strasnedh was broached.

Before the party was due to leave, Dafydd and Christopher spent the night wrapped tightly beneath the furs in Dafydd's bed. Dafydd clung to the king without acknowledging it aloud. He knew that the ghost of Warin was long since chased from Strasnedh, yet in his heart he feared what would be found there.

When morning came they arose together. Christopher went to allow Alain to help him dress while Dafydd donned his clothes alone. Together they descended their narrow stairway and found the traveling party already breaking their fast in the hall.

Once the meal was finished, Patrick stood in close conversation with Marged as she bid him have a care for himself on the journey. She would never dream of holding him back, yet they were still newly married, and she did not like to be parted from him overlong.

Christopher spent a quiet moment with Dafydd before the main hearth, their fingers twined, their heads bent together.

"We will return ere nightfall," Christopher murmured.

"Aye," Dafydd whispered.

"Know that I carry you within my heart," Christopher vowed softly.

"Beunydd," Dafydd replied, "as I hold you safe within mine own heart."

"Always," Christopher whispered.

No further words passed between them as Dafydd accompanied Christopher to the yard, watched as he mounted his horse, and raised a hand to wave as Christopher led the party away. From the battlements, Dafydd watched as the party disappeared from sight, and even though a light rain fell, he remained watching, waiting for Marged to depart from the hall. He knew she wished to keep him occupied as they waited for the men to return, but solitude called him strongly, and he wished to pass the time above stairs in his own stillroom. As always, he found peace amongst the dried herbals he prepared in the small room adjoining his own sleeping chamber.

The same rain that made Dafydd's watch uncomfortable fell upon the king's party. Although they traveled within their own realm, the regiment was still accustomed to arranging themselves as best suited to repel a sneak attack.

Patrick rode at the head of the party with his fast friend and chief advisor, Simon, at his side. During Dafydd's early days with Christopher, Simon fell in with Sir Robert, who was then seneschal, and another squire named Hugh. It had been Sir Robert's plan to besmirch Dafydd's name, yet his plan was thwarted when Christopher himself discovered it. In high anger, Christopher wanted to hang the trio on the charge of treason. Dafydd intervened, and as was his wont, he begged mercy for the men, imparting his wisdom and imbuing into Christopher the peace he carried in his soul. Banished with naught but the clothing on their backs, the men departed and eventually fell in with Warin at Strasnedh. Early on Simon had seen the error of his ways, and when Dafydd was imprisoned in Strasnedh's dungeon, it was through Simon's efforts that Dafydd was rescued and released. Sir Robert met his death during the melee, but Simon returned to Lysnowydh and made his home there. Then, during a short stay in King Henry's court, he was granted his spurs. When the day came for Patrick to depart with Marged and Anwyll to Strasnedh, it was understood that Simon would accompany him. Today as they rode together, they discussed plans for the future.

At the middle of the column, Christopher rode quietly with Sir Richard at his side. It was uncommon for Christopher to be so silent, and Richard allowed him a space of time before he broke the silence between them.

"Your majesty, you knew Dafydd would have no desire to travel this road to Strasnedh."

Startled from his reverie, Christopher gripped his reins tighter, thereby causing his destrier to shy. He reached down and gentled the beast before turning to meet Richard's eye. "Aye, old man, I knew."

"Then what troubles weigh down your thoughts?" Richard asked softly.

Christopher was quiet as he stared through the misting rain at the backs of the riders ahead. At last he heaved a sigh. "You are my conscience betimes, Richard," he said. "Whilst I know Dafydd has no desire to ever lay eyes upon Strasnedh again, I had hoped to convince him to look past his pain, that he might release his hold upon thoughts that trouble him."

"'Tis much to ask," Richard said. "You and I, we cannot know what 'twas like for him. E'en though I am certain you asked him to share, there is likely no way he could make you feel what he felt."

"Mayhap," Christopher said. He sighed again. "Of all the people I know and hold dear, you are the only one with whom I can share these worries." He paused and shifted his gaze to meet Richard's eyes. "I fear Dafydd grows soft. Although his body has healed from the evil brought against him, he shirks his duties as marshal. More and more the duties have fallen to Cuthbert, and Dafydd retreats to his stillroom."

"Have you spoken of this with him?" Richard asked.

"Nay," Christopher said. "Betimes he is fragile, and I wish not to make him feel the worse for things he cannot control."

"Christopher," Richard said, as always making the transition from formality to informality when he judged the moment was right, "you have always known that matters of your kingdom must come before matters of the heart. Lysnowydh is at peace, currently, yet one day the need will arise for a strong hand to guide your troops. Cuthbert has served you long and well, but he is not a leader."

"You are telling me things I already know," Christopher said harshly.

"Be that the case," Richard said, unfazed by Christopher's anger, "then you already know you must needs face Dafydd about his duties."

"The time is never right," Christopher said.

"Nor will it ever be right," Richard said. He watched as Christopher looked away, and saw a muscle tense in his jaw. "What is it he desires?" he asked in a softer voice. "If he wishes not to continue as marshal, then what does he wish?"

Christopher murmured, "I believe he means to hide himself within his stillroom and brew herbals, disengage himself from all outside concerns."

"Dafydd is a gentle soul, Christopher, and long you have known it. If you would permit me to speak my mind...."

"You need no permission, old man," Christopher said, petulance giving way to indulgence. "In truth, e'en if I did not grant you permission, you would speak your mind in any case."

"'Tis truth," Richard said. "Dafydd was well prepared to take over the role of marshal when first you granted him the duty. Skills he had in plenty, and his gentle, even ways were calming to your forces, yet 'tis my belief that the duty has long gone against his grain. Being a woodsman suited him, as he clearly communes freely with the forces in nature."

"Go on," Christopher said.

"Mayhap 'tis time to grant him the serenity of his stillroom. When Patrick and Marged move from Lysnowydh to Strasnedh, grant him the chambers you carved out for their use. Give him the space to work freely with his herbals. Allow him to become healer, as seems to be his true calling. 'Tis my belief he still desires to serve your council, and with him presiding when you are from home, 'twill lighten the load. He will have his hand upon the pulse of your kingdom; he will still play an integral role. In time the turmoil in his mind will fade, just as the hurt done to his body has faded."

They fell into silence again as the words hung between them. The drizzling rain fell harder, and the horses dipped their heads. There was another deep sigh from Christopher before he spoke again.

"Your words have merit, as you knew they did. There remains but one question."

Richard turned to look at Christopher's profile and waited for him to continue.

"If Dafydd no longer serves as marshal, who is to take his place?" Christopher said at last.

"If I tell you my thoughts, you will think I but pushed you thus to further my own gain," Richard said.

"Nay," Christopher said. "I have long known that you never seek to glory your own name."

"'Twas my wish that one of my boys could one day follow in my footsteps and serve you as marshal. My second son, William, has won his spurs and is well past the age of majority. In truth I should have sent him off to seek service in King Henry's court long since, but vanity dictated I keep him at my side," Richard said.

"William," Christopher said. "Aye, I remember him well." He rode in quiet thought for a bit and then said, "I will consider it, yet I would wish to speak with Dafydd first before I displace him from his duties. Mayhap I am wrong in thinking he has no wish to continue as marshal, yet I do not believe I am." He turned to meet Richard's gaze. "I would be pleased and honored to have young William come to serve with my garrison, yet you must know in mine own mind 'twill be temporary. 'Tis still my fervent desire that Dafydd resume his duties when he is ready."

"If 'tis Dafydd's wish to give up the yoke of leadership, mayhap he can be convinced to spend time transferring the reins of power to William. In that way he does not lose face, and William gains valuable knowledge from someone other than his own father." Richard raised a hand to wipe the rain from his face. "And if indeed Dafydd is coaxed to resume his duties one day, William will have gained invaluable experience that will put him in good stead for the future."

"You are wise," Christopher said with a small smile. "Always I have known of your wisdom, yet each time it presents itself, 'tis warming to my bones."

They continued the ride in silence. Close to midday, the outriders reported that Strasnedh was nigh and as yet unoccupied. The rain began to taper off, and all spurred their mounts forward, eager to see what lay ahead.

3
Dark Memories

THE bulk of Strasnedh keep loomed up out of the mists like a derelict shipping vessel on a ghostly sea. The mighty front gate stood open, the doors hanging on broken hinges. Weeds choked the outer bailey, and the outbuildings stood blackened by the fires that had been set once Dafydd was rescued.

Christopher's party rode silently through the destruction, disturbing the occasional stray chicken or scrawny ox as the men passed from outer bailey to inner bailey. The place was clearly still deserted, peopled by the ghosts of those who had once made the place vital. Patrick and Simon sat in somber silence as they waited for Christopher and Richard to reach their position. The soldiers who had accompanied the party hung back to let Christopher confer with his nobles.

"The buildings stand," Christopher said, still mounted on his warhorse. "'Tis only the thatched roofs that must needs be replaced."

"Aye," Richard said. "And yet the outer buildings must be examined to see if they still hold true, else they need to be razed and begun afresh."

"'Tis my hope that the buildings still hold. 'Twould cut the renovations by half," said Patrick.

Christopher cast his gaze about the inner courtyard. "Though you be eager to begin this new life, 'tis my desire the buildings be strong to protect my heir." He smiled to soften his words as he swung from the back of his horse.

"Aye, your majesty," Patrick said as he bowed his head. "'Tis not my desire to be overeager where young Anwyll is concerned."

"'Tis well," Christopher said as he handed the reins to a waiting squire.

One by one the others dismounted, lost in their own thoughts as they gazed at the walls they had last seen in battle. Patrick and Simon moved off toward the stairs leading into the keep while Richard hung back to watch the shifting emotions on Christopher's face.

With Richard trailing in his wake, Christopher circled around to the side of the main building. Here was a smaller, less grand entrance, and Christopher knew that via this entry, the dungeons were accessed. A light breeze ruffled through the narrow passage, stirring the dead stalks of herbs in the neglected kitchen garden. Christopher stood in quiet contemplation for many moments, then turned and found Richard watching from the corner of the building.

"I would see the dungeon," Christopher said.

At this moment, Patrick and Simon rounded the corner and heard the tail end of Christopher's request. Their faces white, they turned to face Richard, deferring to him as the elder.

"'Tis not wise," Richard said. "Naught can come of it; naught can change the course of events."

"Aye," Christopher said with a voice cold enough to match the day and a scowl upon his face. "And yet, I would see it."

"Your majesty," Patrick said, his voice hushed, "I would agree with Sir Richard in this." He paused, uncertain, and then cleared his throat. "There is naught to see save a cold and barren room. In truth—" He faltered, then took a deep breath and continued boldly,

"You are better served by having not seen it the way we did that morn."

A sound emanated from deep in Christopher's chest, an angry growl tinged by the deepest sorrow. "If you will not show it to me, then I will find it on my own. I am not unfamiliar with the way Strasnedh is set inside."

"Your majesty." Simon sidled forward. "I would escort you."

There was a moment of shocked silence as Richard and Patrick turned to face Simon, but Simon kept his eyes fixed only on the king. He trembled slightly, yet was unwavering in his fervor.

Christopher moved toward the small entrance, then turned and raised his hand. "Come."

Holding their tongues, Patrick and Richard watched as Simon strode forward and preceded the king through the small door. Although each shared similar thoughts, they did not speak them as they turned and rounded the building. The inspection must continue.

The air within the narrow passageway was close and smelled of neglect. Stopping long enough to light a torch, Simon turned and raised an eyebrow at Christopher.

"I shall follow," Christopher said tersely.

"Aye, your majesty," Simon said. With the torch held before him, he turned and began the descent down the narrow and ofttimes slippery stairway.

As Christopher followed, he shuddered inwardly at the rustling of unseen creatures in the shadows. In his peripheral vision he noted the differences between this dungeon and the one in his own castle at Lysnowydh. Here the passage was narrow and showed signs that, even in better times, the filth was never removed. Echoed in the stone walls were countless cries of pain and grief.

When Simon stopped, Christopher paused well behind him. The solid wooden door in front of them looked no different from the others they had passed, and yet Christopher felt some affinity with the barrier, as though he would have correctly deduced that this was the room.

Simon set his shoulder against the door, pushed it open, and then fitted his torch within the ring just inside. He turned in the wan light, head bowed, and allowed Christopher to enter the room alone.

Shoulders squared, Christopher stepped through the narrow doorway. With halting steps, he advanced until he gained the center of the room, then stopped and let the feelings evoked by the space eddy around him. In time they overwhelmed him, and he sank to his knees, enveloped in a rush of despair. Unbidden tears welled in his eyes, and a moan escaped his lips. Images flashed upon his mind, and in that one crystallizing moment, he felt the terror and pain that had been meted out upon these very stones. The pain knifed across his heart, and he swayed with its intensity.

Sunk as he was in the overwhelming vortex, Christopher did not hear Simon creep into the room, and was unaware that he knelt just behind him until he spoke. "Have you ever seen a flogging before, your majesty?"

As though he had been stabbed, Christopher flinched. Rather than bite off his answer, as was his wont, he murmured, almost as if sharing with an equal. "As king, I have flogged many miscreants. 'Tis not as much I have seen them as I have meted them out."

"Aye," Simon said, and he continued in a dead voice that forwent the formalities necessary for speaking to his king. "And yet 'tis not the same as watching someone you love and cherish take a beating as was given by that monster."

Christopher sat back on his haunches, his hands clenched into fists as Simon continued with his recital.

"Sir Dafydd was strong, stronger than any man I have ever seen. Each time, when King Warin came upon him, he refused to kneel and give way before him. Silent he was, and defiant as he struggled to his feet, intent upon standing in the face of orders." There was a silence, and then in a voice that cracked with emotion, Simon continued. "He struggled the first time they tried to lead him to the manacles, fought for all he was worth until they clubbed the back of his legs and dragged him across the stones. And he was proud, even though they had taken his clothes the first night they brought him to this hole. The rings bit into his wrists, and they strung him up just enough that only his toes still touched the ground."

After another pause Christopher grated, "Go on."

"The tips of King Warin's whip were studded with steel barbs. Not meant to tear the skin, as the leather did enough of that, but to add increased pain. Most men would cry out and beg for mercy after one lash, but not Sir Dafydd. He leaned in against the wall, clenched his hands around the chains, and swallowed whatever cries of agony built within him. The first time King Warin struck him, the whip split open a mighty weal across his back, painted half his flesh crimson. As he continued, the skin purpled and knotted as the flesh was torn again and again."

The tears that welled in Christopher's eyes spilled one by one, and he was unashamed at their spilling as the awful tale continued.

"Even after the first ten lashes, Sir Dafydd continued to refuse to kneel when his tormentor came into the room. He struggled up, spread his feet wide, and kept his mouth closed. It seemed—" Simon paused to swallow the anger that clogged his throat. "—it seemed that King Warin took perverse pleasure in the floggings. Each time was only ten lashes, but each time some new horror was visited after he was done. Most I did not see, as he did them in private, yet the ones I did see turned my innards so that I lost whatever I had in my belly."

In the silence that followed, both men struggled, Christopher with the images of torment Simon hinted at, and Simon with the knowledge of what he had seen.

"'Twas then, your majesty," Simon said at last, "that I realized I was wrong, and I knew beyond a shadow of doubt that Sir Dafydd was a great man. Evil words said to me by Sir Robert when he was seneschal at Lysnowydh were all lies and jealousy and ignorance. I began to regret any part I had in his torture, I only stayed so as to see if there were any chances to offer him succor or aid. Otherwise I would have abandoned this dark place." Simon drew in a deep breath. "I know no man who could take what he took, your majesty, and that's the God's honest truth. He is that strong and that straight of purpose."

In that final silence, Simon crept out again, leaving Christopher alone in the dark and smoky room. The tears had stopped, replaced by a bitter rage that collected in the pit of his belly. In his mind's eye he could see it, Dafydd chained against the wall, silent in his suffering, proud and defiant until the end.

After creeping along the passage, feeling his way without the torch, Simon came up from the dungeon and stood a moment at the top of the stairway to regain his equilibrium. He wiped at his eyes with the sleeve of his shirt and then stepped out to find the others through the narrow passage that led to the main hall. King Christopher was every bit as tough as Sir Dafydd, and Simon knew that the king would internalize the retelling, and that it would lend to the very fiber of his being.

All were unprepared for the cry of anguish that drifted up through the keep, and they stood rooted to their positions when Christopher emerged into the hall, his eyes blazing with demonic inner light.

"Destroy it," he roared. "The whole of the dungeons must be destroyed." He seemed swollen with the anger and revulsion that coursed through him.

"Aye," Patrick said, as he knew there would be no discussion. "It will be so."

With eyes that still burned, Christopher half ran across the hall, then down the stairs into the courtyard, bellowing for his horse. Richard and Patrick hastened after him and watched as he swung into the saddle and wheeled around.

"Mayhap I should go along of him," Patrick said.

"Nay," Richard said, holding out his arm. "The demons that plague him now will only be settled by Dafydd. Let him go."

⊗⟨ 4 ⟩⊗
Maelstrom

THE rain began again as Christopher raced back down the road towards Lysnowydh. In truth he hardly noticed as he dodged the low-hanging branches. The recitation Simon had given him repeated endlessly in the tired passages of his brain, and now and again a strangled oath issued forth. His horse, well trained for such treatment, never stumbled, although he became lathered with the effort of carrying his rider at such a relentless pace.

When the watchman upon the walls of Lysnowydh shouted that a rider approached at hard pace, the garrison left within the keep scrambled into formation. None were expected back until much later, and it wasn't until the last possible moment that the guards identified it was their king approaching and the mighty portcullis was ratcheted up.

Alain, called from within the keep, rushed forth to take the horse's reins when Christopher leaped from the saddle. Long service to the king allowed him the ability to deduce the reason for the hasty return. Out of breath, he managed, "He's in the keep, your majesty, in his room."

"My thanks," Christopher said, and he turned and rushed inside. It was clear to any who witnessed his hasty flight across the hall that something troubled him deeply.

"What's amiss?" Sir Walter asked hurriedly as Alain entered the hall.

Tipping his head to the side, Alain considered for a moment. His loyalty to the king was strong, and as such he had no wish to talk of the things that he knew plagued him. At last he said, "You must needs tell Agnes to prepare a small supper for the king and Sir Dafydd. They will not be joining the meal downstairs."

"Aye," Sir Walter said, pausing as he clearly waited for more.

At last, moving closer to speak into Sir Walter's ear, Alain said, "All should have known he would come back in this state. He but went to the place where Sir Dafydd suffered greatly. The two are twined deeper than most. 'Tis my belief the king gained some deeper insight whilst there." He paused. "And you'll pardon me for saying, but 'tis also my belief that e'en though he waited above stairs, Sir Dafydd knows this insight was gained."

Sir Walter cast his gaze about to ensure none loitered nearby, and then he spoke softly. "Aye, Alain, 'tis certain you have the right of it." He reached up to touch Alain's arm. "I shall have Agnes send Baldwin to find you when the supper is ready." With that, he turned on his heel and strode away toward the kitchens.

Alain spared one glance toward the stairway and then went off in search of John.

DAFYDD heard the rustling at the door but kept his back turned as he stood at the fire, gazing into the flames.

"Look at me, Dafydd," Christopher said, the anguish clear in his tone. He remained just inside the door, hands clenched at his sides.

"You are early," Dafydd murmured, his shoulders hunched.

"As you knew I would be," Christopher said, and he took one step closer. "Turn and look at me."

Dafydd's shoulders shifted as he heaved a sigh, and then he turned to face Christopher. When their eyes met, torment was mirrored in both, and Dafydd raised his hand.

The urgency returned to Christopher, and he flew across the room to be pulled into Dafydd's arms. Silent, they took comfort from each other until Christopher's shoulders shook.

"My king," Dafydd murmured, "naught can change the past."

"'Tis truth," Christopher said, his voice tight with the emotion that now overwhelmed him. "And yet... I did not know, not like that."

Dafydd reached down to gently cup the side of Christopher's face and raise it that they might meet eye to eye. "I but told you," he said as he stroked Christopher's cheek with his thumb.

"Nay," Christopher said, anger replacing the despair. He tightened his arms around Dafydd's waist. "Telling is not the same as seeing. You but cast yourself forth this day and allowed me to see."

Lowering his hand, Dafydd whispered, "'Twas your choice to enter the dungeon."

A cry was torn from Christopher's lips, and he pushed back. He stood panting with effort before he reached up and unhooked his riding cloak, letting it fall to the floor.

"How is it," Christopher said, desperation in his voice as he worked on his jerkin next, "that you know what I am about when you are not with me?"

"It is as I told you ere you departed this morn," Dafydd said. "A part of me is always within your heart, just as a part of you is in mine own."

Christopher continued to shed his clothing, and as he removed his chausses, he murmured under his breath as though speaking to himself and not to Dafydd. "I must needs make it right, blot out the truth."

"Nay," Dafydd said, locking his hands on Christopher's own. "You cannot strike out the truth. It will always remain." He tightened his hold, feeling the bones in Christopher's wrists nearly break with the force. "Attempt to remove the vision from your mind, yet know that the truth will always remain in mine. 'Tis one of the many things that make us who we are."

With a cry of anguish, Christopher fell upon Dafydd, pushed him back toward the bed, and clawed at his clothes. The indoor slippers Dafydd wore fell from his feet as Christopher worked at the ties of his chausses. The only help Dafydd offered was the unbuckling of his belt, and then he lay quiescent as Christopher continued the attack.

Finally, Dafydd was left clad only in his shirt, a thin shield against the reminder of the scars that crisscrossed his back. He was already hard with desire as he watched Christopher loom above him, hair tousled about his head like the lion Dafydd had always called him.

"I swore an oath to you, Dafydd," Christopher said, his voice gritty, "to love and protect you always. My love you have had in constant from some days before the oath was given."

"Aye," Dafydd said. "And your protection I have had as well. Blot this memory from your vision, and do not chastise yourself for a lack you could not control."

Christopher dipped down, his kiss fierce and hungry as he slid his cock alongside Dafydd's. He reached for Dafydd's hand, twined their fingers together, and transferred the kiss down to nip along the pulse that hammered through Dafydd's neck. "'Rwy'n dy garu di, cariad," he murmured.

Only then did the control Dafydd held over himself begin to slip. Always the king whispered the words of love in English. That he had reverted to Dafydd's native Welsh nearly made Dafydd's heart stop. He pushed up, communicating his need without words.

With his own growl of need, Christopher rose up again, shifted Dafydd's legs wide open, and urged him to hold them up against his chest. Keeping his eyes locked on Dafydd's, he twisted back to reach for the pot of cream beside the bed. He smoothed his creamed fingers over Dafydd's puckered hole while he bent down in one last gesture of tenderness and pressed his lips against Dafydd's cock.

And then the dam broke on his emotions, and he rose up and slammed hard inside Dafydd's body.

Powerful neck arched up, Dafydd opened his mouth and wailed as Christopher held inside him for one long moment, and then he bit his lower lip as Christopher began to move against him.

"Mine," Christopher murmured. "You are mine." His fingers still twined with Dafydd's, he wormed his other hand between their shifting bodies and cupped Dafydd's length up against his belly.

Strong feelings welled between them; words gave way to incoherent moaning. Although Christopher relived the vision painted by Simon's words, Dafydd relived the truth—memories he had unsuccessfully tried to bury on his own. Skin slapped against skin, and the scent of arousal guided his thoughts away from the memory of torture that was always in the back of his mind. Though he had long known that what he had with Christopher was different, this wild joining of their bodies on the heels of the shared vision went a long way in helping him to bury the thoughts with a greater degree of success.

Squeezing Dafydd's hand, Christopher slammed in hard and held. He struggled back and ground out again, "Look at me, Dafydd."

Eyelids fluttering, Dafydd focused and found Christopher's eyes. He shuddered as he felt the pulse of Christopher inside his body.

Although many words swirled inside his brain, the only one that came forth was "mine," and after Dafydd said it, he closed his eyes and released through the king's hand. Tears spilled from the corners of his eyes.

After beginning the motion again, Christopher soon followed Dafydd in release, and he held himself above Dafydd for a long moment once the tremors ceased. When he rolled away, they lay side by side, drenched in sweat and sticky from Dafydd's issue. The silence that fell between them was fraught with words that neither could speak.

5
Decisions Made

WHEN morning came, by tacit agreement Christopher and Dafydd spoke no more of the anguish they had shared the previous night. They rose and dressed and descended the stairs to find Sir Richard breaking his fast, along with Patrick and Simon. Nothing was said of Christopher's abrupt departure the previous day. The men knew upset had prompted it. Talk remained upon safe subjects until Dafydd was called away to the kitchens, where young Baldwin had scalded his arm.

Christopher turned to Patrick and inquired about the results of their trip to Strasnedh.

"The stables must needs be razed and built afresh," Patrick said. "The other outbuildings stand firm. The main building, although scorched in places along the outer walls, is also sound. Of course the main gates must come down and be built afresh, the moat dug again as well."

"How long, do you think?" Christopher said as he pushed his trencher aside.

"I believe we can just raze the stables before winter sets in," Patrick said. "Building the new stable must wait until the snows clear. During the winter months, work can be done on the interior of the main keep. Years of neglect, e'en before 'twas captured, have set all in a sorry state."

"Aye," Richard said. "'Tis true enough. There are men in plenty who will be glad of the work. Many would camp rough in the main hall before the mighty hearth and work through the bitter months. 'Twould save them sitting idle here."

"'Tis well, and I leave it in your hands to make plans. Any of my men you have need of, you may take and direct. Mayhap the sooner you start is the better," Christopher said.

Richard and Patrick murmured their agreement, and when the meal ended, they stood, eager to begin the planning. Christopher rose, reached over, and laid his hand on Simon's arm. "Hold," he said. "I would have words with you."

Simon bowed his head. They waited until the hall began to clear, and then Christopher turned and led Simon to his council chamber. They sat at the main table, before the crackling fire.

"'Tis not my intention to direct young Patrick's hand in the rebuilding of Strasnedh," Christopher said, "and yet it is my hope that you will be amongst those who work there through the winter."

"Aye," Simon said. "With your majesty's permission, he means to put me in charge of the rebuilding."

"'Tis well," Christopher said with a wink. "And when he asks, I will not let on that you have already told me." He folded his hands upon the table. "I would lay a task in your hands."

Simon nodded. "I do not presume to read your mind, your majesty, yet I believe I know the task."

"Aye." Christopher nodded. "You well know the task. I leave it in your hands to ensure the dungeons are filled in with rubble. If Patrick has need of a dungeon, then a new one must be dug." He continued in a soft voice, addressing Simon almost as if he were an equal. "Though I know destroying the room does not change what happened within it, 'twould put my mind more at ease to know it will never be used again."

"'Tis my solemn promise, your majesty," Simon said in a hushed voice, "that 'twill be destroyed as you wish."

In the silence that followed, Christopher stared into Simon's eyes, and then he said, "Though 'twas difficult, I thank you for your words yesterday. Aye, I wished never to hear them spoke, and yet they helped me gain new insight, hearing them in a way Dafydd would never tell me."

"Thanks are not necessary," Simon said softly, "and yet I understand."

"'Tis well," Christopher said. "And now you must needs find the men, that you might pledge your fervor to their mission."

Simon stood and bowed before turning to leave the room.

OVER the next week, a party was formed of men who desired to spend the winter months at Strasnedh, working to restore the keep. True to his words, Patrick did set Simon as the leader of the group. Although he would ride over often to check on the progress, Patrick was needed in Lysnowydh. When the week was at its end, Sir Richard departed for home.

The weather steadily deteriorated as the weeks marched forward to winter. One afternoon, when Christopher returned from patrol, he found Sir Cuthbert drilling what troops remained. Christopher stood for a while, watching, and when the drill ended, he went forward to speak with Cuthbert.

After exchanging greetings, Christopher asked, "Where is Dafydd?"

"'Tis my belief he is within the keep," Cuthbert said.

Christopher nodded. "I thank you for your work with the men. 'Tis well done."

Ruddy color appeared under Cuthbert's fading tan. "'Tis naught, your majesty."

"Mayhap 'tis nothing to you," Christopher said, "but 'tis all to me." He then turned on his heel and strode into the keep.

Inside he found John hurrying across the hall. He walked forward to intersect his path toward the stairs, and John pulled up in surprise.

"I know Dafydd is above in his stillroom," Christopher said. "Would you call him forth and ask him to join me in my council chamber?"

Bowing, John said, "Aye, your majesty," and he ran off to do the king's bidding.

Christopher continued to his council chamber after calling for bread and ale to be brought. He had just lifted his mug to his lips when Dafydd came into the room.

"My king?" he said, and he came forward to sit at the table.

"I have something to ask you," Christopher said. He slid a mug toward Dafydd, "And I pray it does not anger you."

Dafydd set his hand on the handle of the mug and looked at Christopher quizzically. "I know not what you might ask that would anger me."

"It has been eight months and more," Christopher said evenly, "since you were restored to us. During that time, your body has healed and your strength has returned. I know shadows plague your thoughts, and so I wondered if those shadows are what prevent you from fulfilling your duties."

"Beg pardon?" Dafydd said.

"You are more than just my mate, Dafydd; you are marshal of my troops. And yet I find Cuthbert fulfilling your role more oft than not." Christopher held himself rigid. This was a difficult conversation, and he had held it off as long as he might. While he had no desire to turn it into a confrontation, he knew the longer he waited, the more likely that became.

Dafydd closed his eyes and bowed his head.

"'Tis not my desire to upset you, cariad," Christopher said softly, relaxing the formality somewhat, "but you must needs tell me what is in your mind."

"'Tis difficult betimes," Dafydd said.

Christopher leaned forward and took Dafydd's cold hand into his warm one. "Difficult, aye, and yet I have no wish to see you unhappy. I would that you tell me if you desire to continue in the role."

"I desire peace in my soul," Dafydd said softly. "It has been my wish always. When you gave me the opportunity to serve you as marshal, I was glad of it, as it gave me purpose for being here beyond warming your bed. I found I relished the role, and e'en though it went against my desire for peace, leading your troops into battle was far more satisfying than I would have imagined."

After squeezing Dafydd's hand once, Christopher released it and sat back. "Go on," he said.

"Mayhap," Dafydd said, and he paused for so long that Christopher almost prodded him to continue. Before that happened, Dafydd looked up, pain in his eyes. "I am no coward. Naught much frightens me. In battle fear is ofttimes the chiefest enemy, and yet I meet each battle with bravery and vigor."

"Aye," Christopher said. "You are both strong and brave."

"Forgive me, your majesty," Dafydd said, and his voice cracked with emotion. "Imprisonment is a difficult thing. Mayhap you will ever after think me coward, but my imprisonment has made me crave the solitude and peace of mine own stillroom."

Slipping from his chair, Christopher knelt before Dafydd and took both of his hands in his own. "Nay, Dafydd, I will never think you a coward." The memory of Simon's recounting surged up to choke him, and he swallowed hard before he continued. "I have no wish to force you into duties as marshal. I would grant you the serenity of your herbals, and only ask in return that you continue to serve my council." He gazed up into Dafydd's eyes, passion and support evident. "Betimes I know your thoughts before you speak them, and this was one of those times. I love you, Dafydd, now and forevermore, beunydd. If 'tis peace you desire, 'tis peace you shall have."

Tears collected in Dafydd's eyes, and he said hoarsely, "I would not leave your kingdom without leadership."

"And you will not," Christopher said. "I have already spoken with Sir Richard on the matter. His son William is eager to follow in his father's footsteps. I would just ask that you guide him, transfer the reins of power to him slowly, and imbue your wisdom and the peace in your soul on to him, that he might lead the troops with the same grace you have shown." After a short pause, Christopher continued, "I would also but leave the door open, that if one day in the future your mind is changed, the duty of marshal shall be yours again."

Dafydd closed his eyes, and one tear tracked down his cheek. He gripped Christopher's hands tightly. "I have long known of your love, of your caring, yet each time I see it I am struck anew at the immensity."

Christopher rose and pulled Dafydd up into his arms. They stood for a time in each other's embrace.

"In the spring," Christopher said, "Marged and Patrick will move to Strasnedh, taking young Anwyll with them until such time as he is ready to return and begin his training. I would grant you their chambers, cariad, that you might have a stillroom on the main floor of the keep, a place befitting of your skill. I know that more and more the people rely on your healing ways."

"I am truly blessed, my king," Dafydd said softly.

"You are loved," Christopher said.

In time they sat again and shared the bread and ale. Talk moved to safer subjects, and both came away with a fuller understanding and appreciation for the other.

❧ 6 ❧
Peaceful Times

THE winter proved fair, thus aiding those who worked at Strasnedh. Snow fell, but it was often gone within a day. Once each week, Simon returned to Lysnowydh to give his report, and on occasion Patrick rode back with him to see the improvements firsthand. All in all, the work was progressing much faster than had been anticipated, and thus it looked probable that Strasnedh would be ready to inhabit much sooner than originally planned.

Once midwinter passed, Sir William arrived from Sir Richard's stronghold. An instant bond of friendship seemed to spring up between him and Dafydd, and this pleased Christopher greatly. The two men were cut from the same cloth: both were humble yet strong and able to carry out the duties required. Christopher trusted Dafydd implicitly and thus knew William would serve well in his place as marshal.

Although Christopher offered his council chamber that Dafydd and William might talk in privacy, Dafydd preferred they sit before the main hearth. The garrison, confined as they were for the most part during winter, had the opportunity to observe the easy manner with which Dafydd conversed with William, and as such the transition progressed smoothly.

One afternoon, as rain soaked the countryside, Dafydd and Christopher sat before the hearth, sharing a companionable tankard of ale, when William came upon them.

"My apologies, your majesty, Sir Dafydd," he said with a short bow. "'Twas not my intention to intrude upon your leisure."

"Nonsense," Christopher said as he indicated the empty chair beside them. "We speak naught of secrets."

William took his own tankard and sat in the empty chair. "'Tis not fit weather for man or beast," he said. "The men but draw straws for guard duty while the rest spend the time gaming in the lesser hall."

"As long as the guard is set," Dafydd said softly, "'tis well they find something to occupy their time."

"Oh aye," William said. "They know that guard must be stood whether it rains or no."

After some moments passed in cozy silence, Christopher stood and stretched before the fire. "I've a fancy I shall go and check on Marged and Anwyll. Patrick has accompanied Simon back to Strasnedh this day, and young Anwyll seemed troubled with a sore gum yestereve."

Dafydd smiled. "Tell Marged I shall bring a balm for Anwyll's gum. 'Tis likely he but teethes."

"Aye," Christopher said. "I shall pass along your message." With a smile for each, he headed in the direction of Patrick and Marged's chambers.

"If the weather proves clear tomorrow," William said after a few moments, "I shall mount up a patrol."

"'Tis well," Dafydd said. "Like as not, the men have grown weary o'er the past several days of this rain."

"'Tis truth," William said.

"Betimes," Dafydd said, and he rested his tankard upon the arm of the chair, "I but let the captains suggest the need for a patrol, e'en though I knew quite well 'twould be of benefit. Having the idea come from them, instead of me, elevated their own sense of importance."

"And if they do not suggest it?" William asked.

"Then 'tis necessary to guide them," Dafydd said. "When the men feel they are forced to a course of action, they prove sulky and as such are not at their best. They pick at one another, do not give attention where they should. But when they feel included in the decisions, they take ownership and thus are more diligent in their actions."

William nodded. "'Tis sound logic," he said.

"There are times when direct orders must needs be given, and the men keenly deduce when that need arises. In the main, 'twas always my goal to present ideas in such a way that the captains feel included."

"I see the wisdom," William said, "and 'tis what I would ascribe to. Mayhap you might demonstrate?"

"Aye," Dafydd said. "If the weather proves fair in the morning, I shall show you what I mean. I am sure Cuthbert has already anticipated and e'en now sows the seeds amongst the captains."

The next morning William observed as Dafydd laid his plan in motion, and as he had guessed, the captains were already suggesting the patrol before it was brought up. As Dafydd had prophesied, the looks of pride upon the faces of the captains showed they were well pleased to have deduced Dafydd's intention. William made careful note and stored the information away for future reference.

DURING the long winter, Dafydd ofttimes sat before the massive hearth in the main hall, holding young Anwyll on his lap. On these evenings he told stories of the Welsh, tales that had been passed down from father to son over long years. With the cold, those forced to remain indoors crept up to hear Dafydd's rich voice in the retelling of these stories, and while his goal was to share the stories with Christopher's son, in the end he shared them with all.

Over several nights, he shared the story of brothers Lludd and Llevelys. Lludd, the ruler of Britain, found his kingdom was cursed with three plagues, and he sought help from Llevelys, who ruled France by virtue of the fact that he had married the daughter of the king of France, she being his only heir.

Dafydd had already told the story of the first plague, a tale of an infestation of Britain by a faerie race called the Corannyeid. These people were so wise that they were able to hear any conversation held in any corner of the country, even if it was whispered, and thus no harm could come to them. Llevelys had recommended that a certain type of insect be crushed and added to water. The water would then be poison to the Corannyeid, yet the rest of the population of the country would remain unharmed, as they were impervious to the effect.

Once this task was accomplished, the next plague could be dealt with. This plague was a scream that was heard over every hearth of the countryside on May Eve. It terrified the country such that men lost their strength, women miscarried, and children lost their senses. Animals and trees became barren when the scream was heard.

On this night, Dafydd had reached the point in the tale where he began to recount Llevelys's suggestion for freeing the country of this second plague. As he settled Anwyll more comfortably in his lap, he noted that more had come to hear the story, including Christopher, who was lounging in a chair beside him. Dafydd took a deep breath and then began his story.

"Llevelys told Lludd that the second plague in his countryside, the scream that frightened all on May Eve, was a dragon. Another dragon, one from a foreign land, was fighting with this dragon, struggling to overcome it; therefore, Lludd's dragon screamed loudly. Llevelys counseled that Lludd must find the exact center of the Isle of Britain, and there he must dig a deep pit. At the bottom of this pit he must place a vat of the best mead that could be made. A silken sheet must be stretched over the vat."

As always when Dafydd spoke, his lilting voice stilled the baby Anwyll. Even when he was teething or suffering complaints of the belly, he lay still within Dafydd's arms and watched him with great round eyes.

"Llevelys prophesied that Lludd would see the dragons fighting in the form of two large animals, and he said that when these animals tired of their fighting, they would sink down into the pit and be changed into two small pigs." Dafydd bent and pressed his lips against Anwyll's nose before he continued the tale. "When the pigs fell fast asleep, Lludd was to wrap them tightly in the sheet and place them in a stone chest, and then the chest was to be taken and buried deep within the earth."

A log crackled in the hearth, but none moved to shift the embers, as all listened, enraptured by the tale.

"When Lludd returned home, he oversaw the digging of the pit and the making of the mead. He waited until he saw the dragons winging through the sky, fighting fiercely. The scream sent a shiver down his spine, and yet he waited until they tired and fell down upon the silken sheet. Just as his brother had said, they took the form of two wee pigs and fell into a deep sleep when they had drunk all the mead."

Anwyll had long since drifted to sleep. All others still sat in hushed silence to hear the end of the tale.

"Once wrapped tightly in the sheet and locked in the chest, the pigs were taken by Lludd's men to Dinys Emrys, as it was deemed the strongest place in the land. There they were buried, and remained such until Vortigern decided to build his fortress upon the spot many years later." Dafydd shifted Anwyll up over his shoulder, and in a softer voice, he said, "But that is a story for another time. Tomorrow I will continue the tale with the third plague."

For a time all remained seated where they were, still wrapped up in the magic spell of the story. Soon Marged crept forward and took Anwyll off to lay him in his bed. Not long after, the others retreated, giving Dafydd and Christopher the space of the hearth to themselves.

"I find I enjoy the stories, cariad, mayhap more than Anwyll himself," Christopher murmured.

"I had noticed," Dafydd replied.

"'Tis well you keep the culture from which you came alive, for yourself, and also for me," Christopher said.

"I am pleased you take interest in it," Dafydd said. He pushed up from his chair and reached for Christopher's hand. "Come, we must needs retire for the night that the servants who hover at the edge of the hall might find their own beds before the mighty hearth."

Quietly, Christopher stood, took Dafydd's hand, and followed him from the hall.

7
Golden Bonds

BY THE time winter drew to a close, the reins of leadership over Christopher's troops had been fully switched to Sir William. Employing all he had learned from Dafydd, William set about arranging drills, and soon he had fully assumed the role of marshal. In the beginning, Dafydd had watched covertly from within the keep, and as he was pleased with what he saw, he retreated into his stillroom.

The people in Lysnowydh enjoyed the mild weather that winter, and it continued into early spring. Christopher made a final inspection of Strasnedh, and it was deemed fit for occupation. Final preparations were made for the departure of Patrick, Marged, and Anwyll.

Most evenings, when the meal was completed, few lingered in the main hall, as all had pressing duties elsewhere.

"I would have you join me this night," Christopher said to Dafydd as soon as the meal was ended.

"My king?" Dafydd said as he set his knife on the table.

"In my chamber," Christopher said. "I would leave matters of the kingdom for the morrow and bid you leave the comfort of your stillroom. 'Tis my belief that those who depart next week have all the medications they require." He turned with a warm smile. "And I would have you to myself."

Dafydd turned his head and said, "As you wish." The look in his eyes communicated that he was pleased at the invitation. Preparations had dictated that each work long into the night, and as such, each tumbled into his own bed, only to rise early to begin again. When they had time to indulge, it was usually in Dafydd's smaller chamber. Though there was deep familiarity between them, Dafydd never took the honor of joining the king in his own chamber lightly.

Dafydd stood and bowed to Christopher and then made his way up to his own chamber. There, he bathed his face and hands, and disrobed. The warm fur of his bed robe felt good against his skin. He already felt desire coursing through his body. It had been many weeks since he and Christopher had lain together.

Dafydd made his way through the bathing chamber that connected their rooms. A branch of candles stood on either side of the hearth, where a mighty blaze warmed the room.

Christopher sat in his chair before the fire, a goblet of wine in his hand. "Come," he said. "I have poured you a draught of mulled wine."

Dafydd smiled as he took the goblet, and sank into the chair pulled up beside the king's. "Methinks you desire something and you but soften me with this luxury."

Christopher's smile was coy and knowing. He took a swallow of his wine. "Would you believe that what I desire is an evening with my consort in close conversation?"

"Aye," Dafydd said. "Yet knowing you as I do, I deduce 'tis not all you desire. Conversation leads to more, and 'tis my belief the more leads to what you truly wish."

"You speak in riddles, cariad," Christopher said. "You must needs speak freely."

"And spoil the mood?" Dafydd said. "Nay, my king. I would let things flow as they are preordained."

Laughter bubbled up, and Christopher said, "'Tis fair enough." He shifted in his seat, and his robe fell away, leaving a knee exposed. "While 'tis truth that I enjoy conversing with you, I will be honest and admit that it has been far too long since we have shared our bodies. Aye, betimes 'tis just feeling your warmth beneath the furs on a winter's night that will suffice, yet at other times I wish for more." He turned and met Dafydd's steady gaze. "The heat has not left my thoughts of you, sweet Dafydd. You still have the power to make my knees weak."

Dafydd took another drink of the spicy wine and then turned and set the goblet aside. "'Tis not your knees that interest me, Christopher." His voice was a sultry whisper as he leaned forward and rested his hand upon the king's knee. "If I still have heat enough within your thoughts to make your cock hard, then I am pleased."

"You are naughty," Christopher said with a hitch of desire. Keeping his eyes locked on Dafydd, he drained his goblet and set it aside. "You must needs see if you have that heat."

With the firelight bathing them in warmth, Dafydd leaned in closer and slowly moved his hand up the king's thigh, beneath the edge of his robe, and found that he was indeed rock hard. Passing a tongue over his lips, Dafydd sat forward and said softly, "I would not waste time this night with talking, fy llew."

Sitting back in his chair and untying the knot in the belt of his robe, Christopher said, "Then put your lips to a better use."

Massaging with this thumb, Dafydd said, "Wait yet one moment."

When Dafydd released his hold and stood, Christopher moaned softly. He watched as Dafydd shed his robe, turned, and bent forward to blow the candles out one by one. Christopher moaned again as he watched Dafydd's body bending in the firelight. When all the candles were blown out, Dafydd turned and walked back to where Christopher still sat before the fire. He stood for a moment, allowing Christopher to see his arousal, and then he sank to his knees.

"Tell me, anwylyd, what you desire this night," Dafydd murmured.

Goosebumps raised along Christopher's flesh. Dafydd typically said "king" or "llew," the Welsh word for lion, as a term of endearment, but when he reverted to this cherished name, it meant his desire was finely honed. Christopher reached down and cupped Dafydd's cheek tenderly for a moment, aware that tenderness would not return until they were done. Need was high within both, and it was likely they would be swept into a conflagration.

"There are many things I want this night," Christopher said. "I would sink into the warmth of your mouth, brought almost to completion by lips and teeth. And then I would turn you and take you upon your knees before the fire. I would taste your skin and feel you shudder with the force of your release."

Dafydd rose up on his knees, leaned in close so that his lips hovered over Christopher's, and whispered, "Touch me."

With a shiver he could not suppress, Christopher closed his hand around Dafydd's length, tightened his grip until it was almost painful before he stroked up, and then caught Dafydd's lower lip in his strong teeth. Caught in the king's strong grip, he swayed gently on his knees, and when he was released, he sank back down and placed his hands on Christopher's legs.

Gazing up at the king this way was a pleasure Dafydd would never tire of. He drank his fill with his eyes before moving closer to tease his lips over the wide head of Christopher's cock.

"I burn, Dafydd," Christopher murmured, "when you touch me thus."

After circling Christopher's cock with his tongue and pressing his lips against it in a soft kiss, Dafydd opened his mouth and took him inside. He breathed in deeply of the scent of Christopher's arousal, and swallowed to draw him deeper inside.

Christopher groaned and rested one hand on Dafydd's head and gripped the arm of the chair more tightly with the other. He watched Dafydd's lips stretch over his length through half-closed eyes, and his hand tightened once again on the chair when he felt Dafydd's teeth graze over him as he pulled up to the tip.

Long accustomed to what the king liked best, Dafydd continued the assault, soothing with his tongue, teasing with his teeth, and stroking with his hand. When he sank down to the base, he lowered his hand to fondle Christopher's balls, stretched one long finger lower to tease against his hole.

"Ah, cariad." Christopher's words were barely audible on a moan. "'Tis good."

Dafydd pulled up to the tip again, and moving back far enough to meet Christopher's eyes, he carefully ran just the tip of his tongue around the ridged head. Then, as he closed his eyes, he teased his tongue down the underside of his shaft and closed his mouth over the juncture of cock and balls, sucking hard.

Head thrown back for just a moment, Christopher seemed to give in completely to the sensation. Then with a growl, he curled forward. "Enough. You must needs let me have you."

Slowly Dafydd released his hold on the king and deliberately turned to position himself on the furs before the fire. He spread his knees and lowered his head down against his forearms, keeping his eyes on Christopher.

"Wanton," Christopher murmured.

"Want you," Dafydd replied.

As Christopher had intended to take Dafydd upon the furs before the fire, he had left the pot of cream near at hand. He slicked his fingers and bent closer to swipe his tongue down the valley between the halves of Dafydd's ass.

Dafydd groaned and closed his eyes, murmured in Welsh how good it felt.

Only taking the time to slick his cock, Christopher rose up on his knees and pressed against Dafydd's ass. "Are you ready, cariad?" he growled.

"Beunydd," Dafydd moaned.

"Always and always," Christopher crooned. He swept his hand down Dafydd's back. Pressing just the tip inside, he waited for the fluttering to cease before he shoved forward, tawny hair sweeping over his back as he sank all the way inside. "Nef," he whispered. "'Tis heaven inside you."

After just a moment to adjust, Dafydd turned his head again, and his eyes fluttered open. From his angle on the furs he could just make out the curve of Christopher's body behind him, bathed in firelight. It was the calm before the storm. He tightened his hands in the furs.

Christopher twisted to make eye contact with Dafydd for one brief moment before he curled down over his back and nipped at his shoulder. He pulled back and pushed inside again, slowly at first while Dafydd's passage stretched, and then he rose up again. Both hands firmly on Dafydd's hips, he increased the motion.

Unclenching one hand, Dafydd reached up to stroke himself as Christopher slammed against him. Both were balancing on the edge, and through sheer effort of will on both sides, they held out until, nearly at the same moment, Dafydd cried with release and Christopher pushed inside and held as his own orgasm broke.

Leaning heavily upon Dafydd, Christopher eased down against the furs. It wasn't long before the chill in the room touched their overheated flesh, and they rose and retreated to the bed. Christopher turned Dafydd and spooned along his back, curling his hand up to lay it over Dafydd's chest.

"Patrick and Marged depart two days hence," Christopher murmured. "'Tis my wish that you accompany us to Strasnedh. The ghosts are removed, and I would that you face your fears."

"'Tis not fear," Dafydd murmured. He fell silent as he acknowledged what he had suspected in the beginning: Christopher did desire something beyond the wild coupling.

Pressing his lips against Dafydd's back at the end of one of the long scars, Christopher said, "I will be with you, Dafydd, and once this barrier is crossed…." His voice trailed off.

Dafydd grunted softly and said, "I wish not to speak of it, Christopher. It but taints the magic of what just passed between us."

Behind Dafydd, Christopher caught his lower lip in his teeth, but he granted Dafydd's wish. There had been no outright refusal, and it was Christopher's hope that Dafydd would come to see things his way.

8

Bittersweet

OVER the days that followed, Christopher did not speak again of his desire to have Dafydd accompany him to Strasnedh, as he was confident that Dafydd would capitulate. As king, Christopher was used to having people fall into line with his way of thinking, and as he had told Dafydd, the ghosts were gone, purged by the changes wrought in the winter months.

The morning they were to depart dawned fair and clear. Sir Richard rode over from his holding the day before. His purpose was twofold. First he spent time with his son William, and was pleased to see how well he had adjusted in his new role as the king's marshal. It was also his intention to join the party that traveled to Strasnedh, as the whole project had been near and dear to his heart.

While last-minute preparations were made, Richard stood with Christopher and Dafydd in the hall as they all broke their fast. Breads, cheeses, and ale had been set out, and the men stood clustered in groups, eating.

"Dafydd," Christopher said when he had drained his tankard and set it aside, "it is my wish, as I have said, that you go along with us today to Strasnedh."

"I am aware 'tis your wish," Dafydd said, and he drew a deep breath. "But as I have told you from the beginning, I have no desire to ever see Strasnedh ever again."

Anger flared in Christopher's eyes, and his voice was harsh as he said, "Are you a coward?"

Dafydd dipped his head. "Nay, your majesty," he said, "but I remain steadfast in my decision." He looked up again to meet Christopher's eyes. "I but told you two days ago."

"Nay," Christopher said, heedless of the fact that Richard still listened. "Two days ago you but told me you wished not to disrupt the magic betwixt us by talking of it. 'Twas my understanding I had changed your mind."

Sparing one glance at Richard, Dafydd stepped closer that he might speak softly into Christopher's ear. "Then I had the right of it, and you did attempt to bribe me." He turned then and walked away.

Color stained Christopher's cheeks, anger tinged with chagrin that Dafydd had read him so well. "Christ's blood," he murmured.

"Your majesty," Richard said, "you have long known that the very thought of Strasnedh sickens Dafydd."

"Aye, old man, he has said, yet I thought I had convinced him otherwise," Christopher said tersely.

"You are used to all falling in with your desires," Richard said. "You but crook your finger, and your subjects scramble over themselves to appease your desires. Dafydd is a subject, true enough, yet he should be held to different standards. 'Tis not right to expect he will overcome this quickly."

Christopher stood in silence, staring across the hall toward where Dafydd stood talking with Marged. A muscle tensed in his jaw, and his brow wrinkled in a frown. "Aye, Richard, as always, you have the right of it." He paused for a moment, then said softly, "'Tis just—"

"What?" Richard asked.

Christopher hunched his shoulders for a moment, drawn in on himself with his thoughts. There were few who ever heard his inner thoughts, heard him speak as a man and not a king. Though he knew his vulnerability was safe with Richard, it still went against his grain to expose it.

"Dafydd says he does not fear, and I must needs believe it. Ever he has proven that he is fearless, except in this one instance." Christopher sighed deeply. "'Tis my belief he lies to me about this fear."

"Christopher," Richard said gently, "in your realm of experience, I do not believe you can ever imagine what he endured. We have spoken on this before. You would never find yourself in his position, thus 'tis difficult for you to know what 'twas like for him. He is fearless, yes, but when he was held captive he could not help but be fearful."

"There is one thing I can never change," Christopher said, his voice barely above a whisper. "Warin forced my hand. I put duty before my heart, and I fear it will drive a wedge between Dafydd and me. Always he will know that when it came down to a choice, I saved Marged instead of him." He turned anguished eyes on to Richard. "The love I had for Marged at that time paled in comparison to what I felt for Dafydd, what I feel for him now, and yet I left him in the clutches of that monster and rode away with her."

Richard stepped closer and grasped Christopher's forearm, squeezing it tightly. "You had no choice, and Dafydd understands that. 'Twas not just Marged you chose, 'twas Anwyll. Methinks if you had chosen Dafydd that day, he would think the less of you now for leaving Marged helpless in Warin's clutches. 'Tis true that the torture he endured is something neither of you will soon forget, but he was better suited to survive it than she was. 'Tis likely either she or Anwyll would have succumbed and not lived."

Christopher stood, head bowed, as Richard's words washed over him.

"You but make things worse now by asking that he forget all and revisit a place he finds loathsome. Give him time, and understand that it may be that he never wishes to visit Strasnedh again. Allow it, understand it, and do not drive this imagined wedge deeper by badgering him."

"I hear you, old man," Christopher said, and his expression changed from vulnerable to the accustomed mask of leadership. "My thanks."

As he turned away, Christopher locked his fear deep inside his heart. Although he understood the intent of Richard's words, he still carried the knowledge and the worry.

WHEN he walked away from Christopher, Dafydd felt anger and shame warring within his heart. As he approached Marged and Anwyll, he willed the warring emotions away and concentrated on presenting a calm exterior.

"Might I bid your son farewell?" Dafydd asked.

"'Tis as though Anwyll is your son, Dafydd," Marged said as she handed him over.

"In name only," Dafydd said as he took the baby and held him close. "He is of your flesh and will always have the right to call you mother." He caressed Anwyll's cheek with the back of a finger. "I shall miss him greatly."

"I will bring him over to visit you as often as I can," Marged said, "as I am sure he will miss you too."

Dafydd looked up at her, and in that moment communication passed between them that both felt but neither spoke aloud. Marged understood Dafydd's aversion to Strasnedh, where Christopher seemed not to. He reached for her hand and squeezed it gently. "My thanks."

Together they walked from the hall to the bailey, where horses had been brought forth in preparation for the traveling party's departure. Marged's maid, Anne, was already mounted on her horse, and both Dafydd and Marged ensured that Anwyll was well settled with her. As Dafydd helped Marged to her horse, Christopher approached and laid his hand upon Dafydd's back.

"Are you ready?" Christopher asked Marged as she settled into the saddle.

"Aye," she replied with a smile for both.

"'Tis well," Christopher said, and he rubbed a small circle on Dafydd's back. "Might I have a moment?"

Swallowing the ball of anger and shame that still warred inside him, Dafydd turned and said, "As you wish." He followed Christopher to the edge of the courtyard, where the bustle of activity was less.

"I will carry you in my heart," Christopher said.

"My king," Dafydd replied. After a pause he said, "I am sorry."

"Nay," Christopher said, "'tis I who should be sorry. I love you, cariad, always and always."

Dafydd stepped closer so his lips hovered over Christopher's, and he whispered, "Then I shall hold you in my heart as well, and I will wait for your return."

Rising up, Christopher sealed the kiss upon their lips. Although the unsettled feelings remained, there was peace between them when Christopher stood back and called for his horse.

9

Responsibility

ONCE Patrick, Marged, and Anwyll were gone from Lysnowydh, the keep settled into a new routine. All three were sorely missed. Patrick had long made his home in Christopher's household, serving as page and then squire, and his easy nature was missed by the garrison. Marged had not been with them for nearly as long, yet all missed her peaceful manner. Baby Anwyll had inserted himself into the hearts of many, and so even his loss was felt.

Uneasy peace settled between Christopher and Dafydd. Each kept hurt and confusion hidden, and they went about their lives in a pleasant manner toward each other. Sparks still flew between them when they shared Dafydd's bed. For all intents and purposes, the only difference was that Dafydd stayed indoors most days when Christopher worked with the troops.

A suite of rooms on the ground floor of the castle had been modified to suit Patrick and Marged while they lived at Lysnowydh. Individual rooms had been joined together via doorways carved out of the stone walls. Once the rooms received a deep cleaning, they were ready for Dafydd to take them over and make them suitable as an infirmary and stillroom.

Beltane came, and though it was the first anniversary of Anwyll's birth, Christopher decreed the day would be devoted to the celebration of the ancient rituals. As well, he wished for a private celebration between Dafydd and him as they marked the second year of their union. Early in the morning, once the herds had been driven past the embers of the bonfire, Christopher and Dafydd took to horse and rode for the beach. There they spent the day in quiet communion, which did much to repair any hard feelings that remained between them.

As summer drew on, it came time for Christopher to make his annual trek through his kingdom, accepting pledges of fealty and any monetary tributes due him. Talk of the journey started in the council chambers. Sir Walter observed that since Dafydd no longer stood as marshal, he would more easily be able to attend Christopher on the journey.

Christopher saw that the comment was met with stony silence on Dafydd's part, and so he let it pass, having learned from his mistakes.

Shortly after the council broke up for the day, Christopher requested that Dafydd ride with him. He said he but wished to feel the wind on his face, yet Dafydd suspected there was some other motive behind the request.

As they rode near the castle, there was no need for a guard. Dafydd followed Christopher's lead, and soon they entered a forest. Whenever he was amongst the trees, Dafydd felt an inner freedom, and he felt wholly at peace by the time they stopped deep in the woods. Christopher dismounted and looped the reins of his horse over a fallen log. Not waiting for Dafydd, he walked off through the trees.

Dafydd followed after he secured his horse's reins over the same log. In early summer, wildflowers grew wherever the sun touched the ground, and he bent to pluck a yellow buttercup, then twirled it in his fingers as he walked along.

Christopher had stopped at the edge of a hillock where a patch of soft grass grew. When Dafydd joined him, he was sitting on the grass and leaning back against a large boulder. Following suit, Dafydd sat beside him, and for a moment they were quiet as the sound of the forest returned.

"I did not wish," Christopher said softly at last, "to ask you before the council, yet I would wish for you to join me on the trek throughout our kingdom."

Crushing the stem of the buttercup in his fingers, Dafydd said, "I know you wish it, my king, and yet you know I am reluctant to leave the safety of the keep."

"Dafydd," Christopher said as he let out his breath in a long sigh, "'tis well you know that you are safe whene'er you are with me."

"Aye," Dafydd said. He dropped the flower and dipped his head. When he spoke, it was barely above a whisper. "'Tis too soon."

"Will you trade one prison for another?" Christopher turned to look at him. "Do you mean to stay within Lysnowydh keep forevermore?"

"Nay," Dafydd said, and as if drawn by the intensity of Christopher's gaze, he turned to look at him.

Christopher drew a deep breath. "Then you must needs tell me why you will not come with me on the journey, and know that I judge you not." He sat forward and laid a hand on Dafydd's thigh.

A helpless look passed over Dafydd's face, and he stifled a moan that sounded like pain. Christopher moved to gather Dafydd into his arms. He held him close for a long moment, then twisted and turned them both so that they lay back against the boulder. Gently Christopher pressed his lips against Dafydd's brow.

"Your majesty," Dafydd said, anguish in his voice, "I have lied to you. I have told you I have no fear, and yet 'tis not truth."

"Sweet Dafydd, fy cariad," Christopher crooned as he held Dafydd close against him.

"Always the image of Warin is within me," Dafydd said. "I know not where he has gone; I know not when he will reappear. E'en though I know that you are fierce as a lion and protect me always… e'en though I know that mine own body has regained its strength and that none dare test the combined forces of Lysnowydh, there is a part of me that still fears the unknown. Though I would give you all you desire, my king, in this I cannot." He shook in the aftermath of the telling, utterly spent.

A cold feeling settled through the pit of Christopher's belly as he listened, and he tightened his arms around Dafydd when he fell silent. "Never again," he said at last, "must you keep thoughts such as these from me."

"'Tis hard to admit," Dafydd said. "'Tis something that goes against my very grain, feeling fear, admitting cowardice."

"Aye," Christopher said. He reached down and tucked his finger below Dafydd's chin, raised his face to gaze directly into his eyes. "Yet in this admittance, you are stronger in my eyes than ever before. 'Tis a coward that is not able to express weakness. 'Tis truly a strong man that articulates as you just have."

Tears swam in Dafydd's eyes, and his voice cracked as he said, "I am sorry I cannot go along with you, as it pains my heart as well to be separated from you for that long. You are my strength, my salvation."

"Then," Christopher said, "'twill be my charge to finish the journey as quickly as I can."

"'Rwy'n dy garu di," Dafydd said, "beunydd."

Christopher molded his lips to Dafydd's. Each poured all of his heart into the kiss, and it left them breathless. When it broke naturally, Christopher nipped tiny kisses over Dafydd's lips and chin and trailed his hand down to rest upon his hip.

"You make me burn, my king," Dafydd murmured.

Although it had not been his intent, Christopher found he burned as well. They were safe within the woods. Though they had not been accompanied, Christopher knew that his own men watched over him always. Slowly he slid his hand around to lay it against the growing bulge in Dafydd's chausses.

"'Tis not my intent," Christopher said softly against Dafydd's mouth, "that you interpret this as anything more than what it is. I burn as well."

"Aye," Dafydd said as he raised his hand and began to work at the knot that secured the king's chausses.

Together, they worked through layers of clothing until Christopher shifted, slipping down against the soft grass, holding Dafydd to face him. He reached down and caught both cocks in his hand and moaned as he pushed closer for another deep kiss.

Dafydd closed his hand over Christopher's and sighed deeply into the passionate kiss.

There, under the shifting patterns of light dappling through the trees, they rocked against one another until at last Dafydd pulled back, the cry caught deep in his throat. Soon after, he felt Christopher's warm seed coating his hand, and he shivered at the sound of his king's deep groan of release.

Resting against each other for the moment, they were lost in their thoughts until at last Dafydd said, "It won't be forever."

Christopher propped himself up on his elbow, a question in his eyes.

"The fear," Dafydd said as color bloomed over his cheeks.

Christopher wiped his hand upon the grass and rolled over atop Dafydd, pinning him against the ground. "Aye," he said fiercely. "This I know. Yet you must feel in your heart that I understand the source."

Closing his eyes against the intense scrutiny, Dafydd nodded, and the color began to fade.

"Come," Christopher said as he rolled away and stood.

After taking a moment to tie the laces of his sticky chausses, Dafydd stood and followed Christopher back to the waiting horses.

❦ 10 ❦
Love's Warmth

IN TWO weeks' time, Christopher departed on the sojourn through his kingdom. Sir Cuthbert went along with him, as did Alain. This time the first stop was Strasnedh, and after that they went on to Sir Edward's outlying holding. In the first year of Christopher's union with Dafydd, they had skipped Edward's keep on the journey, and this had led to near treason in the kingdom. Now that Edward was back in the fold, Christopher meant to keep him there. Of course, these extra stops added on to the overall length of the trip, but Christopher still vowed to keep the journey as short as possible.

Sir William stood the true test, as he remained behind in Lysnowydh keep and was given his first turn at leadership without the king present. As was to be expected, he passed the test with flying colors, and peace reigned in the kingdom.

With Dafydd at the head, the council continued to mete out justice in Christopher's absence. As he had proven in small matters of everyday life within the keep, he was more than adept at seeing the balance between right and wrong.

While everything moved along smoothly during the king's absence, he was sorely missed. In particular, all could see how Dafydd pined as each day passed. He took his meals in the great hall, presiding at the dais with only William for company. As often as he could, he sat at the fireside after the meal to engage in conversation with any who wished it, but sadness shadowed his eyes. When at last he did climb the stairs to his chamber, it was with a heavy tread born of his obvious dolor. Many times when various castle folk came to find him in his stillroom, he sat gazing off into the distance, as though weighty thoughts troubled him.

Although many felt certain they knew the root of Dafydd's malaise, none felt strong enough to approach him about it. Even Marged, when she brought Anwyll several weeks after Christopher had departed, declined to broach the subject with him.

In all, Christopher was gone six weeks. A sudden summer storm delayed travel between Sir Ranulf's keep and Sir Richard's. Once he arrived at Richard's, he sent forth a messenger to let Dafydd know he would be home within two days. Only then did a spring appear in Dafydd's step.

Showers left over from the storm drenched the king's party as they made their way home, weary from the long trip. Once the outriders were spotted, word was sent in to Dafydd, and he stood at the top of the stairs down into the bailey, waiting and watching with hungry eyes.

As the king dismounted, Dafydd descended the steps and made his way through the puddles. It was not the first time they had been parted, and was not even the longest time they had been away from one another, but the greeting between them was the most intense since their very early days. Heedless of his rain-soaked clothing, Dafydd pulled Christopher into a tight embrace.

"Cariad," Christopher murmured as he returned the embrace. No further words were needed as simply the close contact was enough.

When at last Dafydd broke his hold, he stood back and said, "John awaits above with your bath, my king."

"'Tis well," Christopher said, and he stepped closer, "but I would have you attend me."

A small smile played on his lips, and Dafydd said, "Aye, and yet you must needs stand John. There is still much to settle before I may join you."

"Do not be too long about your duties, Dafydd. I hunger for you," Christopher murmured as he stepped back.

"As do I hunger," Dafydd said with a nod.

Dafydd followed Christopher into the keep, and they parted ways at the stairs that led to their chambers. Dafydd continued on to the kitchens to ensure that a meal was prepared for the returning party and a tray would be sent to his chamber. He dallied in his stillroom for the amount of time he deemed was necessary for Christopher to complete his bath and timed his arrival for the moment the king stood before the fire in the bathing chamber, wrapped in a warmed towel.

"My thanks, John," Dafydd said as he stepped into the small room. "You will find a tray being prepared below in the kitchens; bring it to my chamber. See your father Alain has his rest for the night, as I am sure he was run ragged on the journey as usual."

"Aye, my lord," John said, and he collected the king's clothing. Before he left the chamber, he turned and bowed to the king.

When John had gone, Dafydd turned back to look at Christopher just as he let the towel drop from his body. Still glistening with droplets of water, Christopher turned slightly to let the firelight bathe his body. With a small gasp, Dafydd moved forward, drawn in by the obvious desire that radiated from every pore of Christopher's body. Just as he stepped close, Christopher raised his hand to stop him.

"Hold," he said, his voice a husky whisper, "that I might drink my fill of you."

"Do you wish me to undress?" Dafydd murmured as he stood just out of the king's reach.

"Not yet awhile," Christopher said. "Aye, I missed your body beside mine in bed each night, yet I missed your mind e'en more. You are more to me than just a bed partner."

Warmth filled Dafydd, and he reached out to twine his fingers with the king's. "You are more to me as well, yet I am not made of stone, my king. 'Tis a pleasing picture you present, fresh from the bath and wrapped in a golden glow."

Christopher stepped closer and wrapped both hands around Dafydd's. "Then I must needs wait to enjoy your mind?" He leaned in and pressed his lips against the back of Dafydd's hand.

With a strangled sound low in his throat, Dafydd gritted out, "Please—"

Stepping back, Christopher released Dafydd's hands and backed away toward his chamber. "Come, cariad," he murmured huskily.

Wasting little time, Dafydd stripped from his clothing and lingered long enough to wash quickly before he followed in the king's wake. He found Christopher lounging on the bed, his back resting against the wall at the head, one knee raised, his body spread wide for Dafydd's hungry eyes.

Stalking closer, Dafydd knelt on the bed, crawled up and settled against Christopher's body. Breath let out in a soft sigh, Christopher wrapped both arms around Dafydd's back. "'Tis well," he said as they began to move passionately.

As always when the two had been separated for any length of time, the joining was swift and sweet for having been delayed. Dafydd rose up to bury his face in the crook of Christopher's neck as he came, his muscles shaking with the intensity of release. He shuddered when he felt Christopher's release a short time later.

Subsiding to the bed in a tangle of limbs, Christopher pulled Dafydd close against him and nuzzled at his brow. "E'en though you but showed me how I might stand the time spent away from you, I waited this last week, that I might greet you with all my force. As always, the touch of my own hand does not compare to the touch of yours."

Lips curving into a smile against Christopher's chest, Dafydd whispered, "I had noticed."

"Ah, sweet Dafydd," Christopher said, "I know you have brought food to yon chamber, but I would stay here yet awhile."

"In truth," Dafydd said, "I lack the strength to go and retrieve the tray in any case. Your force has quite worn me out."

Laughing, Christopher slid down so he faced Dafydd. "Would that I could stay right here always. 'Tis where my heart longs to be. Beside you."

"Aye," Dafydd said softly, "and yet you cannot, and I suffer the time away from you with the promise of what just passed between us to keep me warm."

"Ahh," Christopher said as he raised a finger to trace Dafydd's lip, "you missed me."

"Aye," Dafydd said with a catch in his voice. "More still, I regretted my weakness."

"Shh," Christopher said. "Never regret things past that we cannot change. Look to the future and what lies ahead."

"Always," Dafydd said, "your words are a balm to my heart."

"Beunydd," Christopher murmured.

After a time, Dafydd rose and retrieved the tray, and they sat upon the bed and picked at the food as Christopher told of his journey. When most of the food was eaten, Dafydd removed the tray. King and woodsman wrapped together in the furs and settled down for sleep.

The peace and ease between them lasted nearly a month as Lysnowydh basked in the warm sun of late summer. As chill entered the air, the peace was disturbed in a manner none had ever expected.

Summons

AS SUMMER ended there was a decided chill in the air each morning. The air warmed slightly as midday approached, but by late afternoon the chill had returned. The troops at Lysnowydh clung to the warmth, as they knew that soon the inactivity of winter would settle over them all. The indoor servants grumbled as they went about their business, knowing that soon the haven of the keep would be overrun by the men.

Late one afternoon, as the sun crept from the sky, a messenger rode through the outer bailey of the castle. Because he wore the colors of King Henry, he was allowed through without challenge. Christopher was called from the council chamber to receive the message from England's king.

Dafydd watched as Christopher broke the seal on the message, and knew as Christopher's shoulders slumped that he had been called to London. It was not uncommon for Henry to call his vassals in at short notice, yet Dafydd had hoped Christopher would be spared this year. He bowed his head as Christopher folded the message again along the original folds.

"He would see me," Christopher murmured.

"Aye," Dafydd said softly. "'Tis as I suspected."

An unreadable expression crossed Christopher's face, and he turned away. Dafydd watched as he conferred with Sir Walter and then spoke to the messenger. When he was finished, he turned to face Dafydd again. "Come, we must needs finish with the council ere we seek our rest."

A feeling of unease settled in Dafydd's belly at the detached way in which Christopher addressed him. Once they were again seated at the council table, he watched the king covertly, as if trying to deduce his mood. There was one final dispute to settle, and Christopher's voice was well modulated as he meted out justice.

"I have received a summons from King Henry's court," Christopher said as the books were closed for the day. "He expects me within a fortnight."

"Very well, your majesty," Father Geoffrey said. "May we expect Sir Dafydd to stand in your place on the council whilst you are from home?"

Christopher's eyes shifted to Dafydd for a moment, and then he said softly, "I will answer that question on the morrow, when we meet again. I must needs make ready to depart two days hence if I am to arrive when our high king expects me."

"Very well," the priest said, and he stood with a small bow before he led the rest of the council from the room.

"My king?" Dafydd said softly.

His expression still unreadable, Christopher met Dafydd's steady gaze. "This night I would share our meal in my chamber, Dafydd," he said, "away from the prying eyes of our people." He tipped his head to the side. "I trust this is acceptable?"

Dafydd nodded once and stood. "I have duties in my stillroom before I retire."

Christopher nodded and stood as well. "I shall see you an hour hence."

As Dafydd went about his work, the unease grew in his belly. The last of summer's yarrow was removed from the drying racks and carefully put into a stone jar for crushing later. Once the counters were swept clean, there was nothing left to hold him in the sanctuary of his stillroom. With heavy feet, he made his way across the great hall and up the inner stairway to his chamber. He delayed by changing his shirt and then washing his hands and face. At last he knew the king waited, like as not impatiently. Taking a deep breath, Dafydd walked through the bathing chamber that connected their rooms and into the king's brightly lit chamber.

A table had been set before the hearth. Christopher was just pouring wine into the goblets as Dafydd came into the room. He smiled gently and said, "Agnes has sent a dish of sole cooked in wine, roasted beef, a salad of late cress, the last of the peas, and bread with both butter and honey."

"I fear my appetite is slight," Dafydd said as he stood behind the king.

Christopher set the wine decanter aside and swept his hand out, indicating Dafydd should sit. "You must needs eat something, Dafydd. I shall serve you."

Hesitantly, Dafydd sank into his chair. As was his nature, he noticed small things when it came to Christopher, namely the lack of the love word, cariad. Since the messenger had arrived, Christopher had not used the endearment once. When the plate of food was set before him, he hardened his resolve and waited for Christopher to serve himself.

They ate in silence at first, and Dafydd's appetite was tempted by the delicious dishes. When he laid his knife aside and reached for his goblet, he found Christopher watching him steadily, his own meal forgotten for the moment.

"My king?" Dafydd said softly.

"You but know, Dafydd," Christopher responded, "what I wish."

With the sigh caught in his throat, Dafydd set the wine goblet back on the table without tasting it. When he spoke, his voice was husky with the knowledge that Christopher wanted something of him that he was not ready to give. "I know what you wish, and yet 'tis still too soon." He raised his head to meet Christopher's steady gaze. "I would not go with you when you depart for London."

Real pain, as though he had been knifed in the belly, spread across Christopher's face. Whatever anger he felt was suppressed, and between the two of them, he showed the honest disappointment Dafydd's words brought.

"I am sorry," Dafydd said, "nothing has changed. The fears I laid before you at midsummer still remain."

Drawing a deep breath, Christopher said, "And yet you told me you regretted your decision to stay in Lysnowydh when I rode forth on my journey."

"Nay," Dafydd said softly. "I did not regret the decision, only the separation."

The meal remained half-eaten on the table between them. Christopher pushed his chair back and stood. He walked away to stand before the hearth and gazed down with unseeing eyes into the flames.

Dafydd swallowed hard past the lump in his throat and went to join the king before the fire.

As they both gazed into the flames, Christopher said, so softly that Dafydd almost didn't catch his words, "Is this always to be a wedge between us, Dafydd?"

Dafydd flinched as though the words cut across him like a whip. His response was equally soft. "'Twill be a wedge so long as you continue to make it one."

After that, he stepped back, turned, and walked quietly from the room.

Christopher released the breath he had been holding. With effort, he moved his chair away from the table and placed it in the accustomed spot before the hearth. After refilling his wine goblet, he sat in the chair and gazed into the flames, lost in his own whirl of emotions.

Alain arrived some time later, calling softly from the doorway before he entered the chamber. "Are you ready for me to remove the dishes, your majesty?"

Christopher stirred and looked up, then beckoned that Alain join him. "Aye," he sighed. "And you must needs assure Agnes that the meal was indeed delicious. She will but think we did not enjoy it, as we finished only half."

"'Tis well," Alain said. He cast covert looks at Christopher as he moved the plates from the table to the tray. At last, borne of his long relationship with the king, he said, "May I speak freely, your majesty?"

Christopher took a swallow of wine and murmured, "Aye, betimes you are more like my confessor than old Father Geoffrey, who turns up his nose at most of what I do."

The table cleared and moved aside, the tray set on the floor by the door, Alain came to kneel beside Christopher. "'Tis my belief you asked Dafydd to accompany you on your journey to London, and that he refused."

Closing his eyes as he nodded, Christopher said, "'Twas my belief our separation over the summer had done much to change his heart, yet 'twas not the case."

"Your majesty," Alain said softly, "'tis frank words I give you e'en though I suspect they will anger you." He took a deep breath and said, "Just love Dafydd for who he is, a tender soul who loves you more than life itself. Each parting from you tears a piece away from his heart, and you but tear the piece bigger by asking of him things he cannot give." He paused to take a breath and continued before Christopher could respond. "I know that in your heart you fear he holds you responsible for leaving him in that torturous hell and rescuing Marged in his stead, but you wrong him in that, and each time you fight with him, you break his heart, until soon 'twill not be mended." When he had finished speaking, he hung his head and waited.

"Bold words," Christopher said, "and yet acquaintance over time gives you the right to speak them." He reached over and laid his hand on Alain's shoulder. "Think you I should go and apologize, ask him for forgiveness, and tell him that I but wish to never be parted from him?"

"Peace, your majesty," Alain said. "I would never seek to tell you what you should do."

"Aye," Christopher said tiredly. "'Tis but my own broken heart that speaks."

After a moment of silence, Alain stood. "Would you retire to bed?" he asked.

"Aye," Christopher said. He rose and allowed Alain to help him disrobe. "Leave the clothes for the morrow," he said as he reached for his bed robe.

"Aye, your majesty, and again I offer my apologies if I misspoke." Alain turned to gather the tray before he left.

"Nay," Christopher said softly. "You speak naught but the truth, and I am grateful to have you."

Once Alain had left, Christopher stood before the fire one last time. Then, a decision made, he turned and crept quietly from the room and through the bathing chamber, until he stood just inside the doorway of Dafydd's room. He paused to allow his eyes to adjust to the darkness there.

Dafydd was in bed, the furs drawn close around his shoulders. Even in sleep, a look of melancholy covered his features, and Christopher felt tightness in his chest as he perceived Dafydd's pain. Quietly, he shed his robe and climbed in to spoon against Dafydd's back.

"You are mine, cariad," he whispered softly, settling in for sleep.

Through the dream-ridden passages of his brain, Dafydd heard the endearment, and tense muscles relaxed. He melted into the king's warmth, and his dreams eased.

❦ 12 ❦
Harsh Truths

AN UNEASY peace settled between Christopher and Dafydd through the course of the night, and when Christopher departed, the embrace they shared was warm. Dafydd watched from the battlements as Christopher's party rode forth from the keep and was heartened when just as the king reached the verge of the forest, he turned and raised his hand in a final salute.

The journey to London took ten days when conditions were favorable. Christopher pushed the men hard: they rose early each morning and sought rest just after dusk each night. Even for a king, it was not safe to travel the roads after dark.

They arrived in London just as the lamps were being lit on the tenth day of their journey and managed to make it through the main gate before it was closed. The smells of the city assaulted their country noses, and even though all were used to it, they spurred their horses forward that they might reach the relative haven of Westminster Palace. As the palace was situated along the Thames, the fetid air seemed freshened by proximity to water.

Once they arrived at the inner bailey of the palace, Christopher was separated from his men, and he watched with mild envy as they were guided off toward the barracks, most likely to spend the night in camaraderie with the men of the other lesser kings. Although Alain would be allowed to wait upon him for the duration of his stay, he knew this first night would be given to the ceremony afforded him as a trusted vassal. A bath waited, with a courtesan to assist, and if he did not wish to slake his lust, then a meal would be provided in his room. He heaved a sigh as he followed an obsequious servant through the maze of passageways. Lust was in his soul, but it would never be slaked by whoever awaited with his bath. The prospect of a solitary meal and an uneasy sleep was not a pleasing one.

The bath did much to soothe his aching muscles, yet the practiced touch of the attendant only fanned the flames of his desire, and it was with difficulty that Christopher sent her away. Yet again his mind returned to the tired track of wishing he had been successful in cajoling Dafydd to join him. The fine meal laid for him before the fire did little to dismiss the vision of Dafydd, and when he settled into bed later, he imagined that far away in Lysnowydh, Dafydd was dreaming of him.

With morning came the familiarity of routine, and Alain came to assist him with dressing in fine court garb. Many vassals had come from outlying regions, and it was not certain that Christopher would receive his audience with King Henry that day. In some respects, he wondered at the haste that was required when he was summoned to London, as many times there did not seem a pressing need for the gathering.

When he was suitably garbed, Christopher made his way back through the twisting maze of passageways until he found the stairs that led below to the main hall. Many others congregated there, breaking their fast with the bread, meats, and ale set out on long trestle tables. As he ate his bread, Christopher noted that many of those usually associated with King Henry's court were in attendance, as were the French who many complained had overrun the court when the king had married Eleanor of Provence.

Once the meal concluded, the hall was divided. Trusted vassals such as Christopher were guided into an inner chamber, where they congregated in groups until such time as King Henry was ready to give each a private audience. The lesser vassals were expected to remain in the main hall and wait until a general assembly was called.

Based on the service of his father, Christopher was well cherished by King Henry, and he was escorted into the high king's chamber early in the day for his private audience. King Henry was kindhearted by nature and ever generous. Many times his actions came before his thoughts, and he showed the perverse obstinacy of a weak man who was called on to rule when all he longed for was peace.

Christopher bowed low, then placed both his hands in King Henry's as he rose and said, "Your majesty, as always, 'tis an honor."

"Aye, Christopher," Henry said. "It does my heart good to be in the company of those I love best." One endearing characteristic of King Henry was that his left eyelid drooped, giving him a drowsy look, and thus at times making him more approachable.

"I had intended to bring Sir Dafydd along on this trip, that he might enjoy the amenities London has to offer. Alas, I was not able to rouse him from the comfort of Lysnowydh keep," Christopher said as he released his hold on King Henry's hands. "I sorely miss him when I am from home."

The smile left King Henry's face, and soft color crept across his cheeks as he cast his eyes furtively about to ensure they were still alone. "'Tis best you did not bring him, in truth."

"Your majesty?" Christopher queried.

King Henry moved to sit in one of the chairs pulled up before the small hearth in the chamber and indicated that Christopher should take the other chair. "I but gave you leave to handfast with Sir Dafydd because I love you well, Christopher, and I loved your father well before you. Yet surely you know sodomy is a sin, and as such 'twould be my charge to give you over to the Inquisition if you brought him here to Westminster."

Christopher drew his breath in sharply, and he all but snarled as he replied, "Surely you would not, your majesty."

"Aye, I would," King Henry said, and an unaccustomed coldness entered his voice. "I allow you to hold the title of king, when in truth you are naught more than a cock crowing on a dung heap. Lysnowydh, in fact all of Cornwall, is far enough removed from London that betimes I allow you all to move outside of my rule. In truth, those of you residing in Cornwall who style yourself as kings are naught more than simple vassals. In times long in our past 'twas decided that you would bear the title of king, and as I love you dearly, I allow it. But know you this: were you to have brought your shameful proclivities out in the open here, in mine own court, you and Sir Dafydd both would have been subject to Papal Inquisition, and you would not have escaped with your lives."

Most of the color drained from Christopher's face, leaving two spots of red high on his cheeks. He clenched his hands into fists as he sat in mute silence, waiting for the high king to continue.

Sensing Christopher's barely controlled rage, King Henry shifted back and dipped his head as he continued. "I have not shared with Pope Gregory that I have allowed you the dispensation to commit this sin, Christopher, and 'tis best you keep the knowledge to yourself. You have provided yourself with an heir, and thus suspicion is cast away from you. Surely even in your remote corner of my realm, what Thomas Aquinas has writ is common knowledge."

Barely keeping the anger from his voice, and with his hands still clenched into fists, Christopher ground out, "Enlighten me, your majesty."

King Henry shifted in his seat, clearly uncomfortable with the turn the conversation had taken. "All sexual acts that do not lead directly to procreation are a sin against nature." A heavy silence fell between them, filled only with the crackling of the fire. At last King Henry spoke again. "Whilst I believe all Sir Thomas and Pope Gregory have said, I make an exception in your case, Christopher. All I ask is that you do not make it more difficult for yourself, or myself, by bringing that which you must needs keep secret out into the open."

A muscle tensed in Christopher's jaw as he ground his teeth together. He dipped his head and spoke in a deadly soft voice. "In my heart, what I feel for Dafydd is not wrong. How could it be wrong? It galls that I must needs keep it secret, as though 'tis shameful that we have formed such a deep bond."

Shifting once again, King Henry reached over and laid his hand over Christopher's hands where they were clenched in his lap. "Betimes that which we do not understand is the hardest to accept, Christopher. Hear me well, though: Sir Dafydd is not welcome in my court. If the time comes that I make a progression through Cornwall, 'twill be an honor to meet the man who has so ensnared your heart, but until such time, you must needs keep your liaison clandestine."

Christopher slumped forward as the full weight of the high king's words sunk in, and his hands loosened from their fists. He turned, looked into King Henry's eyes, and saw compassion tinged with fear. Releasing the breath he was holding, he murmured, "I hear and understand, your majesty."

"'Tis well," King Henry said with the ghost of a smile. "Go now. We will meet again ere week's end in general assembly."

Christopher rose from his seat and bowed stiffly. "My thanks, your majesty, for this frank talk."

"I know 'twas not easy to hear," King Henry said, "and yet it has been said."

With one final nod, Christopher turned and exited the chamber. The vassals who waited outside pressed forward to draw him back within their midst, yet he waved them off, a scowl firmly fixed to his features.

Alain waited near the door, and Christopher bid him bring his cloak. After it was retrieved, Christopher made his intention clear to his servant. He needed time alone, yet he told Alain where he could be found if his presence was required in court.

With a heavy heart, Christopher walked forth from the castle, through the bailey, until he reached the bitter cold of the main road. Not far from Westminster was a tavern, and there he could nurse the stinging hurt that had been dealt to his heart.

Old Flames Rekindled

A FREEZING drizzle started by the time Christopher reached the Fox. Tucked away along the river, it was a well-trusted watering hole that he had frequented often on past trips to London, particularly in his youth. It was dark and smoky inside, and the midday crowd was swollen with those come to London to be part of King Henry's council. After pushing his way through the crowd and ordering a tankard of ale, he turned to look for a likely roost.

There was an open booth near the smoky hearth, and Christopher slid himself into the seat. Lost in his own thoughts, he was heedless of the smoke that had chased others from the spot. He took a healthy draught of ale, then sat forward and hunched in on himself as he thought back over the morning's talk with King Henry. Although he had long known the church's views on sodomites, he had tricked himself into believing he was exempt from persecution based on the writ of acceptance that allowed him to handfast with Dafydd in the first place. Now he suspected the writ had been solely of King Henry's devising, a method of rewarding a loved vassal while staying on the right side of the church. It was not unusual for King Henry to play both sides of the fence, yet it rankled that Christopher had been caught in the middle.

After taking another long draught of his ale, Christopher sat back against the booth, opened the pouch at his waist, and rummaged through it. He still remembered the day when he and

Dafydd had stood on the beach and recited the vows to one another, the vows that bound them tighter than the simple words Father Geoffrey said the next day during the handfasting ceremony. He unearthed the silver ring, not surprised in the least to find it was warm, as though the silver remembered the moment Dafydd had slipped it over his finger. Usually in London he kept the ring in his purse, not because he feared to show his alliance, but because he treasured it too much to lose it to cutthroats. He smoothed his thumb over the ring and fell into the familiar memory of standing before the forge at the keep the next day, when the castle blacksmith had provided a twin to this ring, one Christopher could give to Dafydd.

Lost in the memory as he was, Christopher did not notice, when the door of the tavern opened, that the freezing drizzle had turned to icy rain. Unaware he was being scrutinized, he picked up his tankard again.

"Christopher of Lysnowydh, you are a sight for sore eyes."

Startled, Christopher looked up into dancing dark eyes, and a smile replaced his scowl. "Nicolas! 'Tis an age since last I saw you!"

"Aye, for certes," Nicolas said as he reached for Christopher's hand. "An age and too long."

Christopher stood and pulled the slighter man into his arms. In his youth, Christopher had spent time in France; Nicolas had been his chief companion and most frequent bed partner. "I had thought never to see you again, given your distaste for the English." He raised a hand to signal that a round of ale be brought to their table, and they took their seats.

"Not all English, cher ami," Nicolas said, his eyes twinkling. "I have quite warm memories of one who sits across this table from me."

"Ah, Nicolas, you flatter me," Christopher said just as the tankards were set before them. "I can guess 'tis Eleanor of Aquitaine who brings you to our fair shore, but I wonder what brings you out from the warmth of Westminster in the rain."

"You, cher Christopher," Nicolas said. "I but arrived in the hall just as you departed from King Henry's chamber, your face downcast. I was surprised to see you, as I know this gathering is for the lesser kings. Does not your father still rule Lysnowydh?"

"Cocks on a dung heap," Christopher said bitterly.

"Pardon?"

Christopher sighed and took a long drink from his tankard. "My apologies, Nicolas. 'Tis not right for me to bring my black mood upon you. My father passed some three years ago, leaving me to rule Lysnowydh. When I met with King Henry this morning, he likened the lesser kings of Cornwall to cocks on a dung heap."

"I am sorry, I did not hear of your father's passing. You have my sympathies." Nicolas tipped his head to the side. "Methinks there is more to the story. I know you well. 'Twould take more than an empty insult such as that to bring on a black mood."

"'Tis a long story, one better left unsaid." Christopher had no desire to share the story with this ghost from his past. The people he longed most to confide in were miles away; he knew he would have to keep the hurt hidden until he was home.

With a Gallic shrug, Nicolas turned to signal for another round of drinks. "Since we are not speaking of it but are speaking of the lesser kings, I have not spotted that old reprobate Warin. Were we to find him, then les trois amis would be complete."

Not able to suppress the shudder, Christopher murmured low under his breath, "Were I never to lay eyes on Warin again, 'twould be too soon."

"Ma foi! What happened to make you say such?" Nicolas said.

Christopher sighed as he sat back against the booth. "Again, Nicolas, 'tis a long story."

"And one better left unsaid?" Nicolas asked. He clicked his tongue against the roof of his mouth when Christopher nodded. "What would you speak of, then?"

"I took a mate some two years past. Although it went against the wishes of my council and the teachings of holy church, Dafydd is my very heart." Christopher rubbed his thumb over the silver ring again and then deposited it back in his pouch.

Clutching a hand to his chest, Nicolas groaned, "Ah, mon cher, you must needs introduce me that I might congratulate him on making such a fine match."

"Then you must come visiting in Lysnowydh. Dafydd but remains at home that he might oversee the kingdom in my absence." Christopher pushed his tankard away and waved off the wench when she approached.

"He has not come with you?" Nicolas waggled his eyebrows and sat forward to speak in a sultry whisper. "I know you well, Christopher. You will not last the week without seeking bed sport, and I shall be ready and able to match you once again."

Hard lines settled alongside Christopher's mouth, and he slid from the booth. "You will find, Nicolas, that I have changed. Gone are the days when you, Warin, and I tripped down the path of debauchery." Raising his hand in mock salute, he continued, "Like as not, I shall see you again ere the week is through, but I would not count on sharing a bed."

Nicolas smiled and bowed his head slightly. "We shall see."

With a smirk, Christopher turned on his heel and walked out of the tavern into the freezing rain.

AS THE week continued, Christopher was able to tuck the hurt he felt deeply away within his soul. In quiet times as he sat before the hearth in his room each night, he acknowledged that his path was set, and as he went against tradition, he must needs accept that he would always be outcast. In truth, he did not need to bring Dafydd with him to London; Dafydd was part of what he considered to be the main part of his life: his kingdom of Lysnowydh. Visits to London were only a sometime part of his life.

In the public times, when Christopher renewed old acquaintances and friendships, he felt the hurt assuaged by good friends, good wine, and good food. They moved in circles, the lesser kings of Cornwall and the trusted vassals from the rest of the realm, and each night there were new faces and new lives to catch up on. Nicolas was about, and though they kept their distance from one another, Christopher felt no animosity.

At long last, the day of the grand council was called, with all the pageantry King Henry could muster. The last of the bitter feelings were dissolved when Christopher was looked upon as spokesperson for Cornwall and thereby afforded the tribute he deserved. Cornwall was peaceful in the main, yet King Henry made it clear that he relied upon Christopher, as the primary landholder, to ensure it remained thus.

When the council was at an end, a grand feast was laid out in the main hall. Christopher found himself seated at a table with the rest of the contingent from Cornwall as well as several members of King Henry and Queen Eleanor's respective retinues, including Nicolas. Talk was kept to subjects of defense within Cornwall's realm and delight in the variety of dishes served. Although Christopher enjoyed excellent food in his own castle, King Henry's kitchens far outshone what he was used to at home. Pastries filled with meats and sauced richly were followed by fish and then roast venison and beef. All was accompanied by wine from France. After devouring the sweets brought at the end of the meal, the men sat back in their chairs, faces flushed and bellies full.

"Tell us of Warin," prompted Edmund, the king of Pennwydh, far in the south of Cornwall. Wine sloshed from his goblet as he raised it to his lips. "'Tis told he faced writ of excommunication and lost his kingdom, yet the reasons why were hushed. All the whispers lead back to you, Christopher. In fact, 'tis said that Strasnedh was ceded to your own kingdom of Lysnowydh."

Flushed with wine and food, Christopher sprawled back in his chair. "'Tis not a secret," he said as he turned his goblet on the battered tabletop. "Warin practiced treason against Lysnowydh. King Henry saw fit to punish him as a result."

"Surely there is far more to the story than that," Edmund persisted. A curling scar on his brow left him with a perpetual scowl.

Christopher eyed the other men who shared the table with him, kings of Tryger and Pidar. They had all served together through many campaigns. All knew Christopher's valor and integrity, and as such he felt able to share the story.

"In the year past, Warin kidnapped the Lady Marged, mother of my heir, Anwyll. When I sought to reclaim her from Strasnedh, Warin bartered a trade." Christopher paused as he took a swallow of his wine. "He bartered in flesh, the return of Lady Marged for my marshal, Sir Dafydd, one very dear to mine heart. 'Twas not easy to extract Dafydd from Warin's clutches, but when we did, we found he had been sorely abused during his stay in Strasnedh."

"For such an affront," Edmund said with a growl, "I would have run him through, left him for dead. How is it he escaped with his life?"

Nicolas sat forward, watching the shifting emotions on Christopher's face.

"'Twas my desire to make him live the balance of his days knowing what he had lost. His kingdom, his very people—nothing was spared once we had secured Dafydd." Christopher drained his goblet and set it down upon the table with a thump. "In truth, if Dafydd had not survived the ordeal, I would have returned to slay Warin, and methinks he but waited for my return."

"And yet your Dafydd healed?" This was offered quietly by Nicolas.

"Aye," Christopher said. "The Welsh have powerful healing magic. He but healed himself."

"Good riddance, says I," Edmund said as he raised his tankard. "I could never hold with Warin's unscrupulous behaviors." He colored slightly, aware of the past history between Christopher and Warin and that likely if he cast aspersions on Warin, they were cast on Christopher as well. To cover his chagrin, he turned and bellowed for more wine. Once the wine had been served all around, he said in a more modulated tone, "If 'tis truth that Strasnedh has been ceded to you, then 'tis well. As good King Henry has fitly deemed, there is none better than you, Christopher, to lead Cornwall."

Christopher raised his goblet to acknowledge the tribute, and talk turned to other matters.

The day had been a long one, and once King Henry rose to seek his bedchamber, the others followed suit. Now that the grand council was over, Christopher did not intend to stay much longer in London. He had already alerted Alain to be ready at a moment's notice to depart for home.

As they walked away from the table, Nicolas fell into step with Christopher. "Light my way, mon cher," Nicolas said. "My chamber is not far removed from your own."

"As you wish," Christopher said.

Once they had passed from the main hall into the passageway, Nicolas drew closer and tentatively reached out to put his hand on Christopher's arm. When his hand was not pushed away, he moved closer still and murmured, "I understand now why the mention of Warin gave you such pain. Your Dafydd must be a strong man to have ensorcelled you so completely."

Warmed by the wine and the intimacy of walking by just the light of a wavering candle, Christopher said, "Aye, none can match my Dafydd." He paused, as he had reached the door to his chamber, and made to hand the candle over to Nicolas that he might continue his journey with the light.

"Mayhap," Nicolas said as he closed his hand over Christopher's on the candle, "you do not remember the passion we once shared, you and I." Using the advantage of surprise, he pressed forward, backing Christopher inside the doorway to his room, away from any that might happen down the passageway. "'Twas magic, mon cher, when we joined our bodies." Snaking his hand up to tangle in the back of Christopher's hair and rising on tiptoes, Nicolas touched his lips to Christopher's in a searing kiss that left them both swaying with the intensity.

Before the kiss could deepen, Christopher regained his senses and pushed hard against Nicolas's chest, sending him reeling back. "Christ's blood," he roared, "by what right do you seek to claim this affront?"

"By right of our long association," Nicolas said as he regained his balance. "By right of the knowledge that you hunger. I can see it in your eyes."

"Know this," Christopher said, and his voice had taken on a deadly chill as he stalked closer. "I hunger for none save the one who waits for me in Lysnowydh. Begone."

"Christopher... cher ami...." Nicolas held up a hand in supplication.

"Nay," Christopher said. "Leave whilst you still can under your own power."

With a lingering backward glance, Nicolas slunk from the chamber.

FAR away in Lysnowydh, Dafydd woke with a start from deep sleep. He sat up in his bed, one hand clutched against the sudden stab of pain in his chest. He was out of breath, as though he had run for a long way, and he hunched in against the pain. Eyes closed, he saw but one vision, that of Christopher far away in London, his lips pressed against those of a stranger.

When cold set him to shivering, he eased back down below the furs, but worry kept slumber from fully returning.

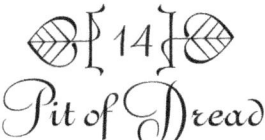

14
Pit of Dread

IN THE morning, Dafydd woke with the pain still lodged in his chest. He rose early, washed and dressed by rote. When John came to assist, he found Dafydd sitting before the fire, pale and hollow-eyed.

"Are you ill, Dafydd?" John asked.

Dafydd was silent, staring with unfocused eyes into the fire. He did not stir until John laid a hand on his shoulder, and then he shook himself and looked up. "Nay, John, I am not ill."

A frown creasing his brow, John removed his hand from Dafydd's shoulder and stepped back. "Would you eat?"

With a small sigh, Dafydd reached up to cover his face momentarily. His voice was muffled as he said, "I would sit beside my hearth yet awhile. If there is need for me in the hall, offer my apologies. I will stir below stairs anon."

"Aye," John said. He stood for a moment gazing at Dafydd's back and then offered gently, "If there is aught I can do…."

After a long moment, Dafydd murmured, "'Twill pass, John. I but saw a shadow in my slumber."

John nodded, then turned and walked from the room. By long association with Dafydd, John knew it was more than just a shadow that disturbed Dafydd's dreams, yet he also knew that to prod Dafydd would send him further within himself.

When Dafydd entered the hall many hours later, all that remained of his malaise was a halting step and a paleness upon his cheeks. As was his wont, he kept to himself, speaking only when spoken to. Although many noted that he seemed downcast, none strove to speak to him about the cause. Those who came to consult him in his stillroom found him reticent, yet capable as always. Once the evening meal was done, he left the hall and returned to his room.

There was no return of the vision that haunted his slumber, and he woke with a firm resolve the next morning. When John came to assist him, Dafydd informed him that they would ride for Sir Richard's keep that very afternoon, just the two of them.

"I would speak with both Sir Walter and Sir William ere we depart, yet 'tis my intention to gain Sir Richard's castle ere nightfall. We will travel lightly. I have no need for court apparel," Dafydd said as he ate the bread John had brought for breaking his fast.

"Very well," John said, noting that Dafydd had regained most of the color in his cheeks.

Dafydd left John to pack, ventured below stairs in search of Sir Walter, and found him hard at work in the king's council chamber. As he was alone, Dafydd sat down at the table with him.

"Might I have a few moments of your time?" Dafydd asked.

"Aye, Sir Dafydd," Walter replied. He tipped his head to the side. "Are you well? Yestereve I thought mayhap you fevered."

"'Twas a passing ailment," Dafydd said. "I but came to tell you that I shall depart in a few hours' time to seek shelter in Sir Richard's keep."

Frowning, Sir Walter sat back in his chair. "It nears the time when King Christopher will return from London."

"Aye," Dafydd said. "You will not be without leadership for long. 'Tis my belief our king will return with all due haste."

Sir Walter noted that the color had drained from Dafydd's face as he spoke, and although they were well acquainted with one another, he did not feel he could pry for the cause of this odd behavior. With a nod, he said, "Would you that I inform Sir William?"

"Nay," Dafydd said. "I will speak with him myself."

Sir Walter laced his fingers together. "And if you have not returned before King Christopher, would you that I not tell him where you have gone?"

After closing his eyes for just a moment, Dafydd said, "'Tis not to be a secret, and I have no doubt that he will inquire. Of course you must needs tell him where I have gone."

"Very well," Sir Walter replied. He watched as Dafydd stood and made ready to leave. "I will send to the stables, have your mount readied."

"My thanks," Dafydd said before he turned to leave.

As he exited the hall to begin the journey through the puddles of the inner bailey, Dafydd observed that John carried bundles toward the stables. Once he had informed Sir William, all that was left was for them to make their departure.

Sir William worked with a small group of captains in the practice yard. The weather was bitterly cold, and their breath rose in clouds of steam as they talked over the drill they meant to run with the squires in the afternoon.

"Hail! Sir William, I require a moment of your time," Dafydd said as he approached the group.

Startled, the men turned. Seeing the look of grim determination on Dafydd's face, William slid from his horse and handed the reins over to Sir Henry. He walked some distance away from the others before he spoke. "My lord? Is there trouble abroad?"

"Nay," Dafydd said. "I but come to tell you that I ride for your father's keep this afternoon. I leave you and Sir Walter in charge until such time as the king returns."

"Is there aught amiss?" William asked.

With a heavy sigh, Dafydd hunched his shoulders forward. "Nay, I but seek Sir Richard's council. As I am sure you are aware, your father is a deep source of comfort for those in need."

William reached out and laid a hand on Dafydd's arm. Though they were good friends, William did not feel he could prod for the true reason for this departure. "Good journey, my lord," he said simply. "Return soon."

"My thanks," Dafydd said, and he reached up to cover William's hand with his own.

Within half an hour's time, Dafydd and John rode forth from Lysnowydh keep. They passed the ride in silence, hunched into their cloaks against the cold. It was clear to John that weighty thoughts tumbled in Dafydd's mind, and yet he knew the thoughts were for Sir Richard's ears alone.

Once Sir Richard's keep was in sight, Dafydd slowed to allow John to ride abreast. "My apologies, John, for dragging you from the warmth of the fireside to accompany me on this sojourn."

"Apologies are not necessary, Dafydd. You but know that," John replied.

"You are loyal," Dafydd said.

"Loyalty is easy with a master such as you," John said.

A muscle tensed in Dafydd's jaw as he murmured, "Mayhap I shall keep you from home for many weeks yet."

"I know not what has happened, Dafydd," John said, "and yet I need not know. I gladly stay by your side, no matter the cause."

"'Tis well," Dafydd said, and he spurred forward to shout up a greeting to the porter.

Although he had not been expected, Dafydd was given a warm welcome. Stable boys came out to take his mount, and he was ushered inside the keep and into Sir Richard's presence. Dafydd greeted the Lady Mary, and then she sent John off with a servant to ensure a wall chamber was prepared. It was evident that something troubled Dafydd deeply, and Richard led him to his council chamber, where a fire burned brightly in the hearth.

"In truth I am surprised you have come visiting on such a brutally cold day, Dafydd," Sir Richard said as he offered a goblet of mulled wine.

"I am sorry to come upon you with no notice, but you once offered me refuge should I need it," Dafydd said as they took their seats. He took the goblet willingly and managed a sip, though 'twas hot.

"My home is yours, Dafydd," Richard said as he folded his hands together. He cocked his head to the side. "When I offered refuge, 'twas during a time when I thought you would need it. What urges you to seek it now?"

"'Tis difficult, and yet there are few I can confide in, Richard," Dafydd said.

"Has Christopher not returned from Henry's council yet?" Richard asked.

A shadow passed over Dafydd's face, and he bowed his head. When he spoke, it was difficult for Richard to hear him clearly. "The Welsh are accused of many things, Richard. Some fears are grounded, others are not. You know 'tis said we are possessed of the second sight?"

Suppressing a shiver at the ominous sound of Dafydd's words, Richard said, "Aye. And I fear not. Whatever such visions might bring you, I am willing to hear them."

When Dafydd raised his head, pain was deeply evident in his eyes. "I have seen a vision in my dreams that whilst in London, Christopher has sought comfort in the arms of another." For two days, whenever the memory of the vision filled his brain, the color had drained from Dafydd's face. Now, as he said the words aloud, scarlet stained his cheeks, and when he continued, his voice cracked. "'Tis my fear that I have driven him away."

"Dafydd, no," Richard said as he sat forward and laid a hand on Dafydd's knee. "'Tis my belief you will never drive Christopher that far away. What, aside from this ill dream vision, makes you think that you have?"

Staring into the depths of his goblet, Dafydd sighed. "'Tis only a year and a little more since...." He hesitated, took a deep breath, and continued. "I need not tell you 'twas a difficult time after I was returned from Strasnedh. In the early days I thought 'twould be easy to put it behind me, yet it proved more difficult than I had imagined. I yearned for the safety of the keep, began to think I had gone soft." Dafydd turned to set the goblet on the table behind him. "In time I realized 'twas just that it has always been in my nature to crave solitude and serenity, things I cannot find easily when out in the world."

"Aye," Richard said. "Go on."

"When Christopher sought to venture through the kingdom on his annual trek, I did not accompany him. It angered him," Dafydd said.

"Mayhap disappointed him," Richard asserted.

"When he returned, I told him I regretted the separation. He misheard my words." Dafydd raised tortured eyes to meet Richard's steady gaze. "When King Henry's summons came, I believe he but thought I had had a change of heart. He asked me to accompany him. I yet again declined. His anger was something I could feel, and e'en though he put a smile on the hurt before he departed, I believe he carried the hurt all the way to London."

"Dafydd, there is much you should know. I am not certain if it will change the pain you feel inside, and yet I would offer the words." He stood and picked up the goblets from the table and reached for the pitcher of wine where it sat just inside the hearth to warm. He poured a measure for each of them, handed one goblet back to Dafydd, and took a healthy swallow of his own before he resumed his seat.

"Here in Lysnowydh, Christopher is a law unto himself. In truth, over many years, he has taken liberties and given himself power that mayhap he should not. Yet his subjects indulge that power, and his vassals admire him the more for it. There are many things that happen here in Lysnowydh which are not accepted elsewhere." He paused for another swallow of wine, and then he said, "Were he to have taken you to London, he would have but run both of your necks into the noose."

With a gasp of surprise, Dafydd exclaimed, "Nay!"

"'Tis truth, Dafydd, and well you know it. Christopher lives openly with you here, and granted, he has writ of approval from King Henry; yet in reality, 'tis not accepted. It may have been his fondest desire to show you off to society outside his kingdom, yet by now he realizes 'twill never be allowed."

Dafydd sat with his head bowed, digesting the information as the fire crackled.

"I know you have but tormented yourself ever since Christopher rode forth from his keep without you. I seek only to assure you that 'tis better you did not go," Richard avowed.

"I understand you, Richard," Dafydd murmured, "and yet it does not remove the vision."

Richard sighed and sat forward in his chair. He laid a hand on Dafydd's arm. "In his youth, Christopher was hard to contain. Many times his father, rest his soul, despaired of ever getting him to settle down. 'Tis a credit to you, Dafydd, that you steadied him, wrought changes that none before you could." He paused, squeezed Dafydd's arm before he continued. "I do not cast doubt upon your vision, Dafydd, but you must needs deduce the meaning. It may not be as you think."

"You say that if I were to have gone with Christopher to London, both our lives would have been forfeit. I have no doubt but you speak the truth. You are much wiser than I in matters such as that. What still remains is that my fear—an unnamed fear that I do not understand myself, hence I know he does not understand it— kept me from doing something he greatly desired." He was silent for a moment, swirling the wine in his goblet.

"Your fear makes him restless," Richard said with unintended harshness. "I seek not to hurt you, only to tell you the truth. You must needs face that fear and put it aside, else what you saw in your vision will become real."

Dafydd drew in his breath, his fingers white on the stem of the goblet. "Would that I could."

"Do not wish it, make it truth," Richard said.

Soon after, one of Richard's house servants came to inform them that the evening meal was served. Conversation was stilted between them as they ate. Lady Mary, sensing that all was not well, refrained from speech. Once the meal was finished, she guided Dafydd from the hall to his chamber and bid him a good sleep.

Tucked in the ample furs and gazing into the brazier that warmed the chamber, Dafydd was awake long into the night, weighing Sir Richard's words.

When morning came he sought permission to stay an additional day, and it was granted. He stayed within his chamber until 'twas time for the main meal. Only then did he emerge, and 'twas clear to Sir Richard that he had made a decision. They ate in silence. When the meal was concluded, Dafydd craved a moment of Richard's time.

"I will leave early on the morrow," Dafydd said.

"I would ask you where you will go, but I have the suspicion you will not tell me," Richard said.

"'Tis truth," Dafydd grunted. "I am certain Christopher will come here to seek me. I did not make it secret from Sir Walter that I came to your home. I do not wish to put you betwixt Christopher and me, and yet I expect he will continue to follow me."

"Then stay here, Dafydd. Stay and face him out. You but know I would give you the privacy you desire."

"Aye, I know," Dafydd said, his face grim with determination, "and yet 'twill be the more powerful if he follows me."

Sir Richard studied Dafydd's face and finally murmured, "As you wish. Just… have a care for yourself, Dafydd."

With only a nod to indicate he had heard, Dafydd turned and walked from the hall.

Chain of Sorrow

SEVERAL days after Dafydd rode forth from Sir Richard's keep, Christopher returned to Lysnowydh with his bedraggled and mud-spattered men. He had cut a full four days off their return journey in his haste to return home. An unsettled feeling had cloaked his every move after he sent Nicolas from his room at Westminster. Now, as he rode into the chaotic press of people in the bailey who had not been expecting his return for a week and more, the unsettled feeling did not abate. With a grim face, he mounted the stairs two at a time, up into the keep.

"Dafydd!" he called, walking across the room with purpose.

Sir Walter hurried forth from the council chamber. "Your majesty! We did not expect you ere week's end!"

"Aye, I made haste with my return." He turned and handed his gauntlets to the squire who trailed in his wake. Although he felt the answer in his heart before he asked, he turned back to Sir Walter and said, "Where is Dafydd?"

"From home this week past," Sir Walter said, a slight flush covering his cheeks.

"Christ's blood," Christopher cursed under his breath, and he turned and began to walk across the hall toward the stairway that led up to his chamber.

"Your majesty, I did not—" Sir Walter sputtered as he followed. "Did you wish I forbid him from going?"

"He has free will," Christopher said over his shoulder. "He is not a prisoner."

"He has gone to Sir Richard's," Sir Walter offered.

"Aye," Christopher said. "'Tis as I expected." He stopped just before the stairway twisted and turned to look back at Sir Walter. "Send Alain, and ask Sir William to wait for me in the council chamber."

"Aye, Your majesty," Sir Walter said.

Christopher continued up the stairs and went straight into Dafydd's chamber. He shivered at the chill in the air, testimony to the fact that Dafydd had been gone for several days. He advanced toward the hearth and stood before the ashes, staring down, trying with all his might to summon an image of his departed mate.

"Dafydd." Christopher's voice was a harsh whisper in the room.

There were no ghosts stirring about. No memories, nothing beyond despair. The unsettled feeling clamored up to choke him, and he knew in his heart of hearts that Dafydd had seen the clandestine kiss, yet likely not the aftermath. He tugged a hand through his hair, and the sound of anguish escaped before he could squelch it. Abruptly, he turned on his heel and stalked from the room, through the bathing chamber, and into his own room, where he found Alain swaying with fatigue before the fire.

"My apologies," Christopher murmured. "I must needs press you to accompany me to Sir Richard's keep in the morning."

"Begging pardon, your majesty. I but thought you meant to ride forth this night," Alain said with obvious relief.

"You know me well, Alain," Christopher said, his shoulders drooping, "and yet I acknowledge that I but pushed hard to gain home in as little time as we did. We must rest this night, set out fresh on the morrow. I but leave you to prepare the bath whilst I go below to confer with Sir William."

"'Tis well, your majesty," Alain said, and he bowed his head and continued into the bathing chamber.

Christopher heaved a sigh, then squared his shoulders and went below to meet with Sir William.

THEY were quiet, master and servant, as they rode forth early the next morning. The fog lay close to the ground, swirling about them as they picked their way along the cliff path. Christopher had averred that they needed sleep, yet his night had been a restless one. It was his firm belief that Dafydd was already gone from Sir Richard's keep, yet he hoped he could squeeze the truth from Richard before leaving on a quest to find him.

When their destination was in sight, the fog began to clear, and just as the guard on the wall identified his king, a watery sun broke through. The creaking of the portcullis and the thud of the drawbridge as it lowered were welcome sounds.

Sir Richard descended the outer stairs as stable boys came forward to take Christopher's mount. His eyes locked with his king's, and there was a moment of silent communication before he stepped forward and folded Christopher into his embrace.

"Come," Richard said simply as he stepped back, turned, and headed back up into the keep.

Christopher followed, and he was aware that no ceremony heralded his arrival, as was tradition when a king visited the keep of a vassal. Even the Lady Mary was conspicuous by her absence as Richard led Christopher to his council chamber. This was to be a meeting of two old friends, not king and subject.

"I have left word we are not to be disturbed," Richard said as he poured a goblet of mulled wine for Christopher, and once he had handed the goblet over, he sank into his own seat.

"He is not here," Christopher said, and it was more of a statement than a question.

"Aye," Richard said after he had taken a sip of the spicy wine. "And yet you knew he would not be."

With a heavy sigh, Christopher set the wine aside untasted. "Why?" he asked so softly that Richard sat forward in his chair.

"I know not what you ask, Christopher," Richard said.

"Aye, you do," Christopher said, a bit of life creeping back into his voice. "You know exactly what I ask of you. Why has he left my keep, and why has he fled when he knew I would seek him here?"

Richard sat back, his long fingers steepled before him. "Even if I had the answers to your questions, you know I could not give them. 'Twas confidence betwixt us whilst he was here."

"I am your king," Christopher growled.

"Aye, your majesty, 'tis truth," Richard said. "Yet even the king can acknowledge that a confidence is a confidence. In truth, you know the answers within your own heart."

With a sound of irritation, Christopher reached for the goblet of wine and took a sip. "Mayhap I know the answers, but I would rather hear them from your lips."

Richard stirred uncomfortably in his chair before he finally said, "As your counsel has been so many times in the past, you must needs begin at the beginning. Did you wish for Dafydd to join you in London?"

"Aye," Christopher said. "And he refused. I did my best to keep my disappointment hidden, and yet he knew."

Sipping his wine, Richard sat in silence, waiting for Christopher to continue at his own pace.

"Betimes I am blinded to reason. 'Twas brought fully to my attention by our lord and master, King Henry, that had I brought Dafydd along, we would have both been taken up by the Inquisition and hung as sodomites." Christopher paused long enough to look at Richard, and a muscle tensed in his jaw as he saw Richard had already gleaned this information. "Bitter words to hear from a monarch I had trusted, one I believed had accepted my alliance and given his blessing by offering a writ that allowed me to handfast."

"Yet," Richard said, breaking his silence at last, "you knew in your heart of hearts that such was not the case, and that yours was a love that would not stretch beyond your own kingdom."

"Mayhap," Christopher murmured, lost in his own thoughts again. "Holding the bitterness in my heart, I ventured forth from Westminster and sought shelter in the Fox, little knowing I had been followed from the palace."

Christopher continued, relating the story of his meeting with Nicolas and the events over the following week that culminated in the grand council. "The council, and the feast that followed, did much to assuage the hurt done to my soul as the lesser kings of Cornwall, though we might be considered cocks on a dung heap by our high king, acknowledged that they look to me for leadership. Mayhap I was full of their praise when I partook of too much wine…."

His voice trailed off, and Richard smiled. "'Tis your wont, Christopher, to go full bore no matter the event. Aye, 'tis truth that e'en back to your father's reign, Cornwall had little place to call their rulers kings, and yet 'twas accepted."

Taking a deep breath, Christopher nodded once and continued. "I must needs ask, though I know the answer, as you have said, in my heart." He paused for a long moment. "Did Dafydd 'see' what came about after the feast?"

'Twas clear a shiver chased down Richard's spine, and all he would say was "I am not sure he saw all, but what he did see was a great trouble to him."

"Christ's blood," Christopher muttered, color draining from his face. He was silent with his own thoughts for a long moment, things he could not share, even with his most trusted friend and advisor. Dafydd's mysticism was one of the things that drew Christopher to him, and yet when it was turned against him this way, it made him uncomfortable, as though he had no secrets at all from his lover.

"Christopher," Richard said as he sat forward in his chair, "'tis betwixt you two, and while I acknowledge that you both but need someone to hear your troubles, I cannot offer advice, nor do I wish to hear the story from your own lips. 'Tis but a small taste of the larger things that bother him. You must needs dig deep within your heart to unravel all of the reasons why Dafydd has fled."

"And yet you will not help me dig into the depths of my heart?"

"Nay, I will not. 'Twill be the more powerful, and have more meaning for you, if you do it on your own," Richard said.

Heaving a sigh, Christopher reached for his goblet and drank down to the dregs before he murmured, "If you knew where he has gone, you would not tell me."

"I do not know," Richard said. "He but stayed with us two nights and then departed ere dawn five days past. I did not ask him where he was going, and knew he would not tell me in any case."

"I will stay the night," Christopher said, "and yet I would not face the members of your household. Let me but sleep in the chamber where Dafydd slept, that I might search in my dreams."

"'Tis well," Richard said.

Because he did not wish to intrude on the everyday business of Richard's keep, Christopher spent the balance of the day upon the battlements. Alain watched him from the shelter of a crenellation, bringing him food and wine near midday. As the sun began to sink, master and servant descended into the hall, where Alain went to join the rest of the servants. Then Christopher was shown to the wall chamber where Dafydd had slept.

As soon as he stepped over the threshold, Christopher felt the difference. In the chamber at Lysnowydh keep there were no memories, no lingering warmth from Dafydd's presence. Here the memories eddied in corners and the furs retained warmth. Christopher tucked himself deep below the covers and stared into the brazier's flames until sleep overtook him.

Dreams did not provide the clues he sought, and when he woke in the morning, although he felt better for having slept the night with the remnants of Dafydd's warmth, he was no wiser as to where he had gone.

After breaking his fast, he bid farewell to Richard. Once on the open road, Christopher informed Alain that they rode for Dafydd's cottage in the woods.

Trail of Tears

A LIGHT snow dusted the forest in the night, and gloomy skies matched the mood of the king as he and Alain rode into the open space before the woodsman's cottage. Christopher shook off the sense of nostalgia that descended over him, and once Alain dismounted, Christopher handed over his reins.

"Do not stable the mounts. Wait. I do not believe Dafydd is here," Christopher said.

"Nay, your majesty, there is no smoke from the chimney. If he was here, he has gone already," Alain said, his head bowed.

The door opened easily when Christopher pushed against it with his shoulder, and ashes in the hearth were testament to the fact that Dafydd had in fact spent time in the cottage, but a quick look around the small interior showed that he was no longer there. Closing his eyes for the briefest moment, Christopher made his silent decision and turned to go back out and join Alain.

"You must needs go back to the castle. I will join you in the morning," he said. "I will seek yet again in my dreams, and when I return, we will venture forth to find him."

"Your majesty," Alain pleaded, "you cannot mean to stay here alone!"

"Aye, I do. Dafydd slept safe here many years before I came upon him. 'Twill be secure enough." Christopher's voice was ragged with emotion.

"Mayhap, yet Dafydd was not king of the realm, your majesty." Alain dipped his head again to show he meant the king no disrespect but had a genuine concern for his safety.

"'Tis peaceful times yet," Christopher said as he stepped forward to take his horse's reins. He reached over and laid his hand on Alain's arm. "I hear and understand your concern, but 'tis not a choice I give you. Go and sleep warm in the castle. Prepare for our journey. We must needs travel light, and yet I know not how long we will be gone."

"Your majesty," Alain said as he raised his head to meet the king's steady gaze, and the rest of what he intended to say dried in his mouth. King and servant had been together many years, and in some ways Alain was given privileges others were not. Because of this, he saw the king's fervor, and so he said, "'Twill be as you wish." Though he still had some reluctance, he turned and cantered toward the track that led back to the castle.

Once the horse was settled, Christopher went inside the cottage and set about bringing the fire back to life. When that was done, he investigated and found a dry crust of bread and a bowl of stale water on the windowsill. He dragged the one chair over in front of the hearth and nibbled on the bread as he sat gazing into the flames. Unbidden, visions of the first time he had stumbled into this modest cottage danced in the recesses of his mind. Though he tried as hard as he could to keep the visions to that first innocent meeting, they slowly slipped out of control, and he relived the first time he and Dafydd had joined their bodies, here before this same hearth.

As the day dragged on, he was able to acknowledge in his heart that Dafydd was not gone for good, but he was unable to put his finger on the exact reasons why he had flown. It was his fervent desire that when he climbed into bed and dreams overtook him, he would find the answers to his questions.

At last, he laid several logs on the fire and went to wind himself in the furs upon the bed. Just as he had experienced in Sir Richard's keep, he strongly imagined he felt Dafydd's warmth still lingering in the furs. As he stared into the flames and began to drift off, he was indeed gifted with a series of dreams, none of them soothing.

"Patrick and Marged depart two days hence. 'Tis my wish that you accompany us to Strasnedh. The ghosts are removed, and I would that you face your fears."

"Then I had the right of it, and you did attempt to bribe me."

Dafydd's face floated above him in the dream as Christopher remembered their conversation.

"'Tis my wish, as I have said, that you go along with us today to Strasnedh."

Even though Dafydd had requested to stay behind, Christopher had pushed again.

"I am aware 'tis your wish, yet as I have told you from the beginning, I have no desire to ever see Strasnedh again."

Christopher's dream moved seamlessly from one conversation to the next.

"You know I am reluctant to leave the safety of the keep." Dafydd's face was woebegone as he said the words.

Christopher tossed fitfully beneath the covers, hovering somewhere between full consciousness and this dreaming. The conversations seemed on an endless loop as they replayed in his mind. Always he attempted to prod Dafydd to drop his fears, his hesitations. Always he was thwarted.

"And yet you told me you regretted your decision to stay in Lysnowydh when I rode forth on my journey."

"Nay," Dafydd said softly. "I do not regret the decision, only the separation."

And still the dreaming continued. He was hot and cold by turns.

"'Twas magic, mon cher, when we joined our bodies."

The kiss burned on his lips. Tossing the furs aside, Christopher sat up in bed, and after a moment, he shivered in the sudden cold. Outside, rain beat against the cottage, and wind blew through the trees. He disentangled his legs from the remaining furs, got up, and shifted the logs on the fire, adding another before he returned to the bed and wrapped himself tightly again.

Although he wished to stay awake, away from the nightmare visions, the sound of the rain lashing the walls eventually lulled him into a more peaceful slumber. The dream this time was calmer, more soothing. There was only the sound of waves on a beach.

When Christopher awoke the next morning, cold and stiff, 'twas with a firm resolve. He took the time to douse the embers within the hearth, and then he went out to saddle his horse and head for home.

Alain waited in the bailey when Christopher rode in.

"Your bath awaits, your majesty," he said as he reached for the reins, "and when you are done, I have food to break your fast."

"'Tis well," Christopher said, "and on the morrow we depart. We will ride through every inch of Lysnowydh until we find him."

Alain followed Christopher into the keep and up the twisting stairway that led above to his chamber.

"I must needs speak with Sir William," Christopher said tiredly as he walked directly into the bathing chamber.

"Begging your pardon, your majesty," Alain said as he came forward to begin the task of undressing the king. "I spoke with him yestereve. He does look to hear from you directly, but he has already assigned a small retinue of men to accompany us, trusted men who will hold their tongues inside their mouths, no matter where we journey."

Some of the worry lines left Christopher's brow, and as he sank into the warm water of the bath, a faint smile played on his lips. "You are more valuable to me than any in this kingdom, Alain. Any save Dafydd, that is."

"Nay, majesty," Alain murmured as he took up a cloth to bathe Christopher's back.

"Aye," Christopher said firmly. "'Tis the very fact that you do not see it that makes it so."

Christopher spent the balance of the day in quiet introspection, breaking only to meet with Sir William and take the evening meal in the hall. When at last he laid his head to sleep, it was only the sound of waves on a beach that filled his dreams. Old memories began to swirl over the sound, and the kernel of an idea began to form, but it would take more than a week for the kernel to blossom.

❦ [17] ❦
Empty Hands

IN THE end, Christopher was delayed in leaving the keep for another day. Although Sir William was well trusted and Sir Walter was more than adequate in his role as seneschal, both admitted they would welcome the support of Sir Richard, as it was unclear how long Christopher would be away. Loath to admit it, even to his trusted advisors, Christopher felt some sense of relief that his kingdom would be left in the good hands of his oldest friend.

It was a somber party that departed in the gloom of early morning. Peace reigned within Lysnowydh and all of Cornwall, but it was not seemly for the king to travel with only his body servant. The men selected to accompany them were well seasoned, and all were well known to Dafydd. It was not Christopher's intent to come upon him with a regiment and drag him back to the keep, and as such he made it clear to all that it was a friendly party that rode the countryside, even though in his own heart he became more desperate with each passing day.

This trip differed from Christopher's summer journey through his kingdom in more than one way. During summer months, the group frequently dallied between stops, camping out and sleeping beneath the stars. But the nights were bitterly cold in the dead of winter. As such, the party rode hard from one place to the next, most times leaving well before dawn and arriving as dusk settled across the land. They were not expected, and yet they received warm welcome from each keep they visited. Even though worry sped his feet, Christopher spent a few days with each vassal so as not to offer insult to any.

As they entered the second week of travel, Christopher's patience was sorely tried, and he found it increasingly difficult to keep civil. It didn't help that this struggle only brought thoughts of Dafydd more strongly into his head. He clearly remembered a time when he first traveled with Dafydd upon this very road. Though the inhabitants of Lysnowydh accepted that their king had formed an alliance with another man, Christopher deemed that he would not force them to accept the act under their very noses, and thus he refrained from joining his body with Dafydd's whilst they slept in the keeps of his vassals. Night upon night of the lovers being separated wreaked havoc upon Christopher's soul, and he snapped at Patrick, then a young squire, for little offense. Dafydd came to the rescue and correctly deduced the cause of Christopher's peevishness. After that, Dafydd instructed Christopher in the fine art of pleasuring himself, that he would not work himself into that state again.

Shaking himself from his reverie, Christopher sped his horse forward. He saw that they approached Sir Mortimer's keep, and thus the outer boundaries of Lysnowydh. Desperation choked him as they clattered across the lowered bridge into the inner bailey. Sir Mortimer himself greeted them as they came to a stop.

"Ho! King Christopher! What brings you so far from home in the midst of winter?" He raised a hand to help Christopher dismount.

With a heavy sigh, Christopher dismounted and said, "You have given me the answer I seek by such a greeting." A muscle tensed in his jaw as he watched the rest of his party slide from their mounts. As Sir William had promised, the men in his party were circumspect, and no word of the real reason for their journey had been whispered abroad when they stopped. Wishing to keep it that way, Christopher leaned in to say to Mortimer, "I would tell you in confidence."

Sir Mortimer's keep was small, and because his council chamber was shabby, he led Christopher in to sit beside his huge hearth. With their chairs pulled up close to the roaring fire and a small table between them to hold their tankards of ale, they were indeed isolated from the rest of the keep's inhabitants.

"By virtue of the fact that you do not know why I have come, I know this is yet another dead end," Christopher said. He rested his head on his hand as he gazed into the mighty hearth. "Sir Dafydd has gone from Lysnowydh keep; I but seek to find his trail."

"Sir Dafydd? I have not seen him since he was rescued from that cur Warin, may he rot in hell with all the denizens thereof," Sir Mortimer said, and then, as if catching himself, he added, "Warin, that is, of course, not Dafydd."

In spite of his melancholy, Christopher smiled at Mortimer's bluster. They had been acquainted long, and one of the things that had always put Mortimer well in Christopher's good graces was his direct, albeit blunt, manner. "Warin rots in a hell of his own making," he murmured as he reached absently for his tankard.

"Begging pardon, your majesty," Mortimer said. "I would not badger you for reasons you would not give as to why Sir Dafydd has flown from your keep, but what causes you to seek him here in my humble corner of the world?"

"I know not where he has gone, and I promised him once that if he sought to fly, I would hunt him down to the ends of my kingdom. As for the reasons why he has fled, e'en that I am not sure of. I only know he has gone." Christopher stretched his feet closer to the warmth of the fire and sighed deeply.

"Aye, well and true, all of that." Mortimer turned to take in Christopher's profile. "But why seek him in your own kingdom?"

Frowning slightly in consternation, Christopher turned to face his companion. "Pray explain yourself."

"Again I beg your pardon, my liege, but if something has occurred that angered Sir Dafydd or frightened him, would you not suspect he would leave our shores for his own? Would you not expect him to return to Wales?"

A sound of anguish escaped from Christopher's lips, and he bent forward, head in hands. This eventuality had not occurred to him, and he acknowledged in agonized silence that the sound of the ocean he heard each night in his dreams might very well be waves lapping on the side of a ship headed for Wales, not breaking on the shore of Lysnowydh's coast.

"I do not feel it," Christopher murmured at last.

"Majesty?" Mortimer leaned in closer.

Shaking his head and pulling his emotions back into check, Christopher said in a firmer voice, "In my heart I feel he is somewhere within Cornwall. This was not my last hope; there is still Godfrey's keep." He tightened his hand into a fist on the arm of his chair. "Dafydd has told me there is naught remaining in Wales for him."

"Sir Godfrey's keep is a godforsaken place," Mortimer snorted as he sprawled back in his chair. "None would seek haven there, as 'tis literally the end of the world."

"Mayhap," Christopher said. He unclenched his fist and reached for his tankard. "E'en though I have come upon you unawares, I beg shelter for the night."

"Of a certainty, your majesty. My Lady but readies the solar for your use." Sir Mortimer stood. "Would you that I leave you in solitude until the meal is served?"

"You know me well, old friend," Christopher said gratefully, and he did indeed sink deeper into his thoughts once left alone.

By the time the meal was at an end, a cold chill swept through the keep. Rain lashed the walls, blown in from the west. Christopher knew he disrupted the sleep of Sir Mortimer and his lady by taking their solar bed, yet sunk in melancholy as he was, he did not care. Wrapped tightly in the furs and staring into the depths of the smoldering fire, he drifted into slumber.

Dreams descended, fueled by the raging storm outside. Hazy images of the woodsman's cottage in the grip of a snowstorm caused Christopher to toss irritably in his sleep and murmur that Dafydd was not there, he had already checked. The next memory that invaded the dream was a miserable trek through the rain to Strasnedh after Warin had been ousted, a trek where he was kept company by the memory that he had but pushed Dafydd again to come out of his shell, made Christopher moan in his sleep.

As dawn approached, the nightmares calmed, and he once again was lulled by the sound of the ocean. Cloudy images began to form, and even though he slept, he held his breath as the swirling visions solidified. First, a stretch of beach that was vaguely familiar. Next, a lone figure wrapped in a cloak, stooping to pick through the debris left by the storm. Finally, an inn perched on a cliff. When the three images merged into one, Christopher sat up in bed and gasped as he released the breath he was holding. Clutching the furs against his chest, he shivered in the early morning cold and made sense of the dream. Dafydd was sheltered in the village below Sir Godfrey's keep.

Slowly easing back down in the bed, Christopher curled in on himself and waited for the dawn.

⊗{ 18 }⊗
Hearts Asunder

BY MORNING'S light, Christopher had locked his emotions tightly away. When Alain came to assist him, Christopher informed him that he intended to ride forth that very morning for Sir Godfrey's keep, and that he planned to leave the men behind. He did not even reveal to his trusted body servant that he felt certain Dafydd was at the inn in the village, because he knew that if his visions had played him false, he would be crushed. Best to suffer that hurt without an audience.

Sir Mortimer, although surprised, agreed he would keep the king's men but avowed that if no word had come of Christopher's safe arrival in Sir Godfrey's keep by the end of the second day after Christopher left, he would send his garrison to seek him on the road. As had been the case the previous day, Christopher was somewhat comforted by Mortimer's blunt manner.

After a small breakfast of cheese and ale, Christopher bid Mortimer and his men farewell and rode off with only Alain accompanying him. The storm, having blown itself out during the night, lent a freshness to the air. Christopher felt his hopes rising, and he struggled with the knowledge that it was still likely his hopes would burst.

As they neared the coast, the terrain grew rockier, and Alain was forced to fall back and allow the king to ride ahead. Conversation had been light between them but was now nonexistent.

Just as the sun reached the high point in the sky, Sir Godfrey's keep became visible. Christopher spurred his horse forward, though ever mindful of the rocks, and he felt his hopes reach a zenith when he saw the portcullis sliding up before they were close enough to be identified. It was likely they were watched for, and that could mean Dafydd was nigh.

Indeed, when Christopher and Alain rode across the drawbridge and found Sir Godfrey waiting, it was certain the quest was at an end. Christopher was not able to hold back his cry of relief when John stepped forward from Sir Godfrey's shadow to reach for the reins of his horse.

"I am glad to see you, your majesty," John said, his voice breaking with relief.

Ignoring Sir Godfrey for the moment, Christopher enveloped John in a bear hug, and his own voice broke as he said, "'Tis well."

"We have expected you lo these many weeks, your majesty," Sir Godfrey said.

Releasing his hold on Dafydd's body servant, Christopher turned and reached out a hand to Sir Godfrey. "If 'tis so, then why have you not sent word?"

"He requested we not send to you," Godfrey said. "And e'en though I owe my fealty to you, in truth, I owe it to Sir Dafydd equally. He requested sanctuary. I gave it. In truth, 'twas my belief that eventually either you would come of your own accord or he would relent and allow me to send to you." As he spoke, Godfrey reached for the rosary beads that hung at his waist, as if to cast off the knowledge that Dafydd did indeed commune with the other world. "Would you come inside and rest?"

"He is not here inside your keep, Godfrey," Christopher said, and though he phrased it more as a statement than a question, he still waited for Godfrey's response.

Tightening his grip on the beads, Godfrey shook his head.

"Then I would have words with my servant and take leave to join him."

"As you wish," Godfrey said, and he bowed his head. "Should you have need of aught, you have but to ask."

"On the morrow, send to Mortimer's keep. Ask that my retinue depart and abide here within your walls until I return," Christopher said.

"'Twill be as you wish, your majesty," Godfrey said. "Godspeed." He turned and made his way across the bailey toward the stairs that led up into his keep.

When they were alone, Christopher turned toward John. "'Tis my belief Dafydd is below in the village."

"Aye," John said as he sank to his knees before the king. "I beg your mercy, majesty. In truth, I but asked Dafydd to allow me to send for you, and he refused. I wished to send word he was whole and well, and yet he remained firm in his belief that you would find him."

Christopher bent and gently cupped John's cheek. He raised John's face that their eyes might meet. "You need not treat for mercy from me, John. You serve Dafydd well and are loyal to a fault. Your father has much to be proud of in you."

Alain reached down and took his son's hand. He helped him to his feet. Whatever words he had to say to John would be saved for when they were in private, but the look in his eyes told that the king was indeed right: he did feel pride in his son.

"I would go to Dafydd now, ere the sun sets," Christopher said. He turned to face Alain. "I would leave you here to wait for the men. In truth, I know not how long I may stay at the inn with Dafydd. 'Tis my hope we do not wear out our welcome here in Godfrey's keep as you wait for me."

"'Tis likely, with your permission, he will find work for the men whilst they wait," John said quietly. "In truth, he has housed me grandly these weeks past. I would go with you now that I might set the room at the inn to rights. 'Tis none so comfortable in winter months."

"'Tis well," Christopher said. He turned to remount his horse while John swung up on Alain's mount. "Bear my apologies to Sir Godfrey that I have left so abruptly."

"Aye, your majesty," Alain said as he dipped his head.

Within half an hour of arriving, Christopher rode forth with John, down the well-worn track toward the village. There still remained a few hours of sunlight, and clouds sat off the coast, ready to bring more rain to the sodden countryside.

When they arrived at the inn, John dismounted first. "I will but see to the room, your majesty, and bring your horse with me back up to the keep. You have only to send, and I will return. 'Tis most likely Dafydd is not in his room, as 'tis his wont to walk upon the beach by day."

"Aye," Christopher said as he slid from his horse's back. "'Tis as I expected. My thanks, John." He turned and began to walk toward the beach.

Once he was clear of the cluster of buildings, Christopher's steps faltered. Before him, in the distance, he saw a lone figure wrapped tightly in a cloak. As Christopher watched, the man stooped down, appearing to examine the debris left behind by the recent storm. Emotion welled up inside Christopher, and he knew the exact moment when the distant figure felt his presence, because he stood slowly and turned toward him.

Time seemed to freeze as Christopher continued on, and Dafydd began to walk toward him. When they were close enough to see each other's faces clearly, Dafydd let go of the tight hold he had on his cloak, and Christopher groaned aloud as he quickened his pace.

Without pausing, they walked into one another's arms. Christopher buried his face against Dafydd's solid chest and felt himself caught up in a strong embrace. For moments, neither man moved. They stood on the sand and let the breezes eddy around them. There was no need for words, and indeed emotion clogged their throats.

At last, loosening the strong grip but not releasing his hold completely, Dafydd stepped back that their eyes might meet. He saw tears welled in Christopher's eyes, and he bent and touched his lips gently to his cheeks. "Anwylyd."

At the sound of the endearment Christopher knew Dafydd reserved for times of strong feeling, the tears spilled over, and Christopher drew in a ragged breath before he rose up to claim Dafydd's lips in a deep, bruising kiss. Only then did Dafydd tighten his hold again.

When at last the kiss broke, leaving each breathless, Christopher found his voice. "Why, cariad?"

"I would not have this conversation here, my king, where prying eyes may see and curious ears may hear," Dafydd said. He stepped back at last, found Christopher's hand, and held it tightly.

"But I would not be private with you, Dafydd, not now." Christopher raised his free hand to dash across his eyes, angry with himself for letting the fear, concern, and worry come forth in this manner. "I would but hurt you with the force of what would transpire between us."

"No more pain than has already been caused," Dafydd said, his voice harsh.

Christopher tightened his hand on Dafydd's, and his own voice was harsh as he responded, "Physical pain, Dafydd, from the force of my body against yours."

Dafydd dipped his head, flexed his hand to dislodge it from the king's grip, and said, "Physical pain I do not fear, not from you, Christopher. 'Tis the tumult in mine own soul that must needs be addressed first."

Wincing, Christopher took Dafydd's hand again. This time the grip was gentler. "There are no easy answers, cariad, but mayhap I can give my word to listen first, before the physical need o'ertakes me."

"'Tis well," Dafydd said.

With their hands still clasped in the gentle binding, Christopher turned to walk back toward the village, and Dafydd stood still, pulling Christopher back toward him. A slight frown marring his brow, Christopher watched as Dafydd reached into the pouch that hung at his waist and extracted a seashell.

"I found this yestereve, as the sun began to set. 'Twas proof that you were on your way to me."

When Christopher took the shell, he drew in his breath. It was tinged softly with pink inside, and tears welled in his eyes again as Dafydd's words washed over him.

"There was anger in my soul, my king, when I left Lysnowydh keep. So much anger that I left mine own shell in my chamber. When I found this one, I knew the anger was misguided."

Christopher looked up from the shell and saw that tears stood in Dafydd's eyes as well. The shell was a symbol, a talisman that Dafydd carried with him. Once, he told Christopher a story about finding such a shell and presenting it to his mother, only to have it lost as they walked back from the beach to their home. After the telling of this memory, Christopher had searched the beach until he found such a shell, and then he presented it to Dafydd. The shell had taken on strong meaning for Dafydd, and he carried it with him the day they handfasted.

The enormity of the breach between them loomed high above them, and Christopher swallowed against the lump in his throat. No further words were spoken, and they began to walk together toward the inn.

Tumult

THE room at the inn was much as Christopher remembered it, except that the bed was stripped bare and a pallet had been laid on the floor in front of the hearth. In the short amount of time John had been in the room, he had added furs and blankets to the pallet, built a roaring blaze in the hearth, and set a tray of food covered with a cloth on a low table by the door.

Most of this Christopher noticed in peripheral vision as he watched Dafydd remove his cloak. So many things crowded in his mind he feared he would explode. Although he had promised to listen first before his emotions overcame him, he advanced toward Dafydd, reached for his arm, and wrenched him around that they might see one another face to face.

"Why, Dafydd? Why did you run from me?"

Dafydd pulled away but found he was held tightly, so he loomed closer, using the advantage of his height. "Why did you kiss another, Christopher?"

Christopher pushed back and then slammed Dafydd against the wall. "And how do you know this, from a dream?"

Dafydd shoved against Christopher but found he was held tightly against the wall. He grunted, "Aye."

"Then your dream vision played you false, Dafydd. You did not see what came after that innocent kiss."

"It matters not what came after." Dafydd's face grew red with anger. "What matters is that your lips touched another's."

With a strangled cry, Christopher pulled Dafydd toward him and began to yank roughly at his clothing. "'Tis my right to refuse to explain further, Dafydd."

With equal fervor, Dafydd tore at Christopher's clothing until both stood naked before the flames. In a brutal dance, Christopher swept his leg behind Dafydd's and toppled him to the furs. Knees on either side of Dafydd's body, he reached up and tangled his fingers through Dafydd's short locks. Pulling on Dafydd's hair, he angled his head back, leaving his neck exposed.

"You are mine, Dafydd," Christopher ground out as he bent down and touched his lips to Dafydd's neck.

Growling low in his throat, Dafydd reached up and put strong hands around Christopher's hips. With little effort, he reversed their positions so that he had Christopher pinned against the furs.

There was no softness. Too much time had passed, too many misunderstandings. Dafydd pinned Christopher against the furs with a strong arm, stroked a hand down his leg, and pulled it up, held it back. With soft, growling moans, he dipped his fingers in the pot of cream that John had left near the hearth and closed his teeth over Christopher's nipple. Shifting their bodies, he found Christopher's entrance and thrust his fingers inside.

Christopher's struggles subsided; he arched his back and wailed loudly when Dafydd's fingers found him. Through the fringe of his eyelashes, he watched anger, desire, and despair cover Dafydd's face, lit by the firelight. The rough fingering lit the fuse of desire inside him, and he pushed up against each nearly vicious thrust. There was no need for words; this fierce communion of bodies was enough.

Teasing with teeth and then soothing with tongue, Dafydd worked on Christopher's nipple until he felt his inner muscles relax. Only then did he pull back and make eye contact through the growing darkness in the room. Pausing long enough only to swipe a fingerful of cream on his aching length, he lined up, and as he sank inside, his eyes slipped closed. The heat and tightness of Christopher's passage were enough to make him shudder, and in truth he felt the answering shudder of Christopher's body below him.

As he reached down to close his fist around Christopher's cock, he opened his eyes, leaving his soul naked to Christopher's gaze. Running his tongue over suddenly dry lips, he croaked, "Anwylyd."

Christopher stirred and raised both hands to reach up and grip the back of Dafydd's head. His voice broke as he whispered, "Cariad."

Gripping Christopher tighter, Dafydd pulled out and slammed against him hard, moving him against the furs and the pallet below them. The tenderness of the endearment melted away as all the frustration he had carried in his soul began to spill over into the urgency with which he took Christopher.

Outside, the storm began to swirl around the inn. Drafts snuck in through cracks in the mud walls. The sound of skin slapping against skin, the grunts of the men entwined on the floor before the hearth, and the wail of the wind combined to overwhelm all.

With a final hard thrust, Dafydd pushed inside and held as he climaxed into Christopher's passage. Christopher released his hold on Dafydd's head, lowered one hand to join Dafydd's on his cock, and flung the other above his head as he stroked Dafydd's hand until he felt his own release. He forced his eyes open again to watch Dafydd's face, saw the silvery track of one tear as it slid down his cheek. Only then did he recover his strength, surge up, and wrap both arms tightly around Dafydd's neck.

Although the storm lashed the window and the cold began to wrap icy fingers around their overheated flesh, Christopher and Dafydd sat locked in each other's arms, each breathing in the scent of the other, until at last the shivers were not leftover tremors of release, but testament to the bitter cold.

Dafydd eased away, let Christopher sink down on the pallet and pull the furs about him. After turning away, Dafydd levered another log onto the fire, and then he settled down beside Christopher. Under the furs, Christopher found Dafydd's hand and twined their fingers tightly together. Too spent from the wealth of feelings that had spilled between them, they drifted into a light doze and finally a deep sleep.

By morning the winds had subsided, but the rain still fell outside the window. Dafydd stirred first, waking to find that Christopher clung to him in his sleep. He disengaged himself carefully and then stood to use the chamber pot in the corner. When he returned, he found Christopher curled on his side, watching him. Dafydd tended the fire and then turned and said, "Are you hungry?"

"Aye," Christopher said. "Yet I would not eat yet awhile." Then he stood and went to use the pot. When he returned, he said, "I would hold you."

Dafydd gave a final poke to the log, and then he sank back down to the pallet and held up a hand toward Christopher. Spooning against him facing the fire, Christopher waited while Dafydd tucked the furs about them both, and then closed his hands over Dafydd's arm, holding it tightly. They were quiet, listening to the hiss and crack of the new log settling into the fire, and the drip of rain just outside the window.

"I love you, Christopher," Dafydd murmured against the back of his head, his palm flat against Christopher's chest.

"As I love you, beunydd," Christopher replied. He fitted his fingers between Dafydd's. "Our bond is a lifelong bond."

"Aye," Dafydd whispered.

Christopher bent his head and pressed his lips against Dafydd's wrist. "I asked you yestereve, and you did not answer, cariad. Why did you run?"

"I believed in my heart that you perceived weakness in me. When you left for London, I was left with the icy fingers of doubt in my heart and not the warmth of your love. Too many times in the recent past I have felt your disdain." Dafydd's voice remained strong as he spoke.

"Nay, Dafydd, nay, I do not perceive you as weak, I but knew eventually you would get past what transpired," Christopher said as he pressed his hand hard against Dafydd's. "And you have never had my disdain."

"Mayhap, and yet I am still left with doubt, and I still know your heart. E'en though you say 'tis not disdain, I feel it keenly."

Christopher pushed his fingers down below Dafydd's, curled them in against his palm. "I am the king, and yet I am only a man. Mayhap I believe that if I close my eyes, the terrors will all be removed. I push too hard because I want you always by my side, Dafydd. Always, beunydd."

Dafydd bent his head to press a kiss upon Christopher's shoulder. "'Twas my intent to prove to you that I can get past the weakness."

"What was the cause, aside from this misguided need to prove something to me that I already know?" Christopher asked.

"The dream, which you dispute, where I saw your lips touch those of another." It was as he said these words that there was a telltale crack in his voice.

Tightening his hand on Dafydd's, Christopher said fiercely, "I do not dispute it, Dafydd. What you saw was correct. Soon after I arrived in London, I renewed my acquaintance with a ghost from my past. Although he sought to rekindle what was once between us, I staunchly refused. 'Tis in the past, and as you said yestereve, it matters not that I was in a high fury when I sent him from the room for his cheek, that I made haste with my departure, even tempting King Henry's wrath by leaving before permission was given."

"You had the right of it, my king; I did not see those things. The shock was great. I felt it as a physical pain, and it prodded me out of the fear I hid behind," Dafydd murmured. "I knew I must needs put distance, a greater distance, between us, that I might prove my worth."

Christopher was silent as he listened to the desperation in Dafydd's voice. In many ways, he did not know how to assuage the hurt, how to fix the problems between them, and though he knew time would heal the wounds, he was impatient and not willing to wait. At last he twisted in Dafydd's arms that he might face him and said, "Why here? Why this far?"

Color flushed his cheeks at the close scrutiny, and Dafydd knew that Christopher saw straight into the depths of his soul. "I knew you would seek me at Sir Richard's keep and that if I retreated to my cottage, you would find me there as well. This is the greatest distance from Lysnowydh keep, and is a place where you and I once came to an understanding. In time I but cast myself into your dreams that you would find me here."

"Sweet Dafydd," Christopher said. He rose up on his elbow and gazed down into Dafydd's face. "I once told you I would hunt you to the ends of the earth if you ran from me. Despair was heavy upon me as I searched." He paused to take a breath. "Know this: 'tis not that I feel I own you, 'tis that you own me. Life without you would not be worth living."

Tears rose in Dafydd's eyes, and he reached up to cup a hand around the back of Christopher's head, eased him down for a kiss. Both knew that the hurt was not completely smoothed between them yet, but a different emotion rose as the kiss deepened.

Christopher pressed his thumb against Dafydd's cheek in a gentle caress and moved so that he settled between Dafydd's legs, their cocks nestled together, swelling against one another. Dafydd spread his legs wider and reached down behind Christopher's ass, pulling their bodies more tightly together.

"I would feel you inside me, Christopher," Dafydd murmured.

In answer, Christopher leaned down for another kiss, pressing his tongue against the seam of Dafydd's lips, gaining entrance. He shifted that he might reach between their bodies and tease gentle fingers against Dafydd's hole.

Once Christopher shifted, Dafydd reached down and began to stroke Christopher's length lazily as they reacquainted themselves through the kiss. There was urgency in both, but the edge had been taken off the previous night, and now they took time to savor.

As Christopher pushed just the tip of one finger past the tight ring of Dafydd's muscles, Dafydd tightened his grip slightly and pulled up to the tip. Breaking from the kiss, Dafydd turned his head to the side and moaned with desire and need.

While reaching for the pot of cream, Christopher nibbled kisses down Dafydd's neck. When he pushed two fingers inside, he groaned with the increased pressure of his cock in Dafydd's fist. He gently rocked his fingers inside, stretched them as he pulled out. He rose up on his knees with a gasp as he pulled away from Dafydd's warmth.

"Look at me, Dafydd," he murmured. When Dafydd's eyes fluttered open, he said, "'Rwy'n dy garu di, cariad, beunydd."

Dafydd's mouth opened, but no words issued forth as he was overcome. He kept his eyes open as Christopher sank deep inside of him. This was a gentle lovemaking compared to the wildness of the previous day, yet the release when it came was more satisfying.

Their hunger was forgotten as they twined together in the aftermath.

❦ 20 ❦
Honesty

AFTER a drowsy morning, the lovers woke at midday. Dafydd went below stairs in search of warm water for bathing. He returned with a tray containing a basin, two bowls of passable mutton stew, and a flagon of sour wine. Once they had bathed their faces and hands and dressed in warm clothing, they sat before the fire and attacked the bowls of stew with gusto. Each watched the other covertly until at last Christopher spoke.

"The bruise is not healed yet."

Startled from his reverie, Dafydd looked up. The corners of his mouth rose in a wry smile. "Mayhap."

Sighing, Christopher reached for Dafydd's empty bowl and set it aside. He refilled their goblets and took his seat again. "'Twill take time, and yet I believe 'twill come."

Dafydd raised the newly refilled goblet to his lips and drank. "Aye, last night you said your life would be worthless without me, and 'tis much the same for me. The hurt will be healed, mayhap sooner than later."

Rain still pattered against the window, keeping them trapped in the room as the shadows lengthened. Christopher reached out and laid his hand across Dafydd's as it rested on the arm of the chair. Although they had slept through the night and most of the morning, a heavy tiredness weighed down their souls. Both acknowledged silently, in this stilted conversation, that the wounds would heal, and each was willing to give the other the space needed.

"This rain brings in warmer weather," Christopher said at last. "Soon winter will depart for another year." He stretched his feet out toward the fire. "I believe we must needs seek outside Lysnowydh for new squires this year. We will need to rebuild our troops soon."

"Peace still sits upon the land," Dafydd said, "and yet you have the right of it. 'Tis not good to become complacent."

"There were rumblings at King Henry's court," Christopher said, "that the peace might not last. Within the past year we have lost several squires. Many have risen through the ranks, and the sweating sickness that settled upon the outlying regions claimed more than its fair share. 'Tis well we bolster our garrison that we protect our own."

"There is that, and the need to strengthen the garrison at Strasnedh as well," Dafydd said, his voice cracking upon the name of the hated keep.

Christopher turned to study Dafydd's profile. "Aye," he said slowly.

Dafydd turned, soft color staining his cheeks as he said, "Anwyll must needs be well protected. In truth, Patrick is capable, yet I would that the garrison there be fortified."

While squeezing Dafydd's hand, Christopher said, "'Tis well, and you have the right of it: the garrison there is our first priority." Although he longed to assure Dafydd again that 'twas little likely that Warin would return to his old stronghold, he did not wish to tear the healing wounds asunder. "With spring comes Beltane," he said, changing the track of their conversation, "and Beltane brings two things to celebrate."

"Anwyll's second year and the renewal of our vows." The shadow had left Dafydd's face. "I relish the thought of both."

"As do I," Christopher said. "This year, 'tis my intent that we spend Beltane day in quiet communion, you and I, away from the keep."

"Were the choice mine," Dafydd murmured, "I would spend the day in the woods, mayhap sleep in my cottage that night."

"Aye, mayhap," Christopher said. "I had thought the hunting lodge. A private retreat, just us two."

"'Tis your choice," Dafydd replied.

Conversation died out after that as both sat in the warmth of the fire. Outside, the sun went down, the wind picked up and the storm started in earnest again. Soon, Dafydd added another log to the fire, and when he sat back to watch the flames begin to lick around it, he said, "I would sleep."

"Aye," Christopher said.

They rose and disrobed, settled down upon the pallet again, bodies spooned together under the furs. Christopher shifted close and pressed a soft kiss on Dafydd's cheek. "Sleep well, cariad."

In answer, Dafydd pressed a hand against Christopher's back and held him close.

WITH morning came a break in the clouds, and wan sunlight filled the room. After dressing and breaking their fast with bread and cheese, Dafydd and Christopher descended the stairs.

"I must needs send word to Godfrey's keep," Christopher said as they stepped out into the street.

"Aye," Dafydd said. "I will have the innkeeper send his son. 'Tis how I keep in communication with John."

"Let them know I would stay here with you yet awhile," Christopher said. "I have no pressing desire to return just yet."

Once the instructions were given to the boy, the two men set off on foot toward the beach. Although the storm had passed, there was still a chill in the air, and few were around to encounter the king in such an unlikely place.

They walked along the beach for quite a long ways, until they reached the edge of the natural inlet and a rocky promontory. Here the breezes eddied about them, and, hunched in their cloaks, they perched upon some rocks. After a while, Christopher reached absently for Dafydd's hand and tucked it within his own.

"E'en though, as we said yestereve, the bruise is not healed yet, I would tell you of my time in London," Christopher said.

Dafydd squeezed Christopher's hand and continued to look out across the water.

"As is his wont, King Henry urged me to London with great haste. Though he granted me private audience soon after my arrival, I spent much time in idleness for far too long until he deemed it time for his grand council." Christopher was quiet for a moment until Dafydd turned to look at him. He took a deep breath and went on. "There are few in the world that I might confide in, Dafydd, and in fact you are the only one I may speak with and be sure that what I say will remain in confidence."

"Aye, my king," Dafydd said as he raised his arm to open his cloak and let Christopher settle in beside him.

"I wanted you with me, Dafydd. I am sorry to tear the healing wound afresh, but I wanted to take you with me to King Henry's court, that I might share the abiding love I hold for you within mine heart for all to see. I longed to share the luxury of life in Westminster with you. Mayhap I wanted to see it all anew through your eyes." His voice became harsh with the telling. "I also wanted to have your warmth beside me in bed each night, as Westminster is large enough to house me in private chambers."

Listening in silence, Dafydd kept an arm tightly around Christopher and let him pour out his heart.

"'Twas not to be, nor likely ever to be. Our high king tore that dream asunder with his proclamation that our love, the love that has made my world whole and right, can never be shared outside our own kingdom. 'Tis to be something dirty, a thing that men only mention in whispers, something for which I should feel shame. Were we to be seen together anywhere other than Lysnowydh, we would tempt harsh recrimination. 'Tis likely we would be hung only after being disfigured by those who do not understand that love such as ours is not only possible, 'tis right. We are sodomites, Dafydd, considered no better than men who slake their lust with animals."

Dafydd felt Christopher trembling under the protection of the cloak, and he wrapped his arms more tightly around him. A lump had formed in his throat, and he felt unable to respond.

"Aye, in truth I knew the rest of England felt this way. 'Twas but my own misguided perception that because he granted us leave to handfast, King Henry accepted our liaison. In that, I was sadly mistaken." Christopher turned in toward Dafydd, pressed his cheek over Dafydd's chest.

"Christopher," Dafydd said, his voice breaking past the lump in his throat, "in truth I had never thought past our own world of Lysnowydh. 'Twas Richard who enlightened me. Mayhap 'twas my own error, I but knew, e'en before I felt your touch, that our destiny was together. I told you that visions of you filled my dreams, and my heart quested to find you until at last I did. 'Tis simpleminded of me, I know, and yet I know that what is betwixt us is not wrong, is not shameful."

"Aye," Christopher said, "'tis not. 'Tis just that my heart broke when I heard the words from King Henry's mouth, and then I had not even the balm of your touch to take the hurt away."

"I am sorry," Dafydd whispered.

"Cariad," Christopher said, "I tell you this not to make you feel sorrow. 'Tis just that I want nothing hidden betwixt us."

"'Tis best," Dafydd said, and he drew a heavy breath as he sensed that there was more to be revealed.

"His name was Nicolas," Christopher said. "A ghost from my shared past with Warin."

Dafydd tensed, and before he could pull away, Christopher clamped an arm around him.

"Hold, Dafydd," Christopher said, his voice hard with command. "Listen, and we will speak of it no more."

"'Tis difficult," Dafydd said, his voice ragged.

"None of this is easy," Christopher said, "and yet we bear it because we must. He came upon me as I but attempted to drown my disappointment after the meeting with King Henry. I knew, Dafydd, when I first laid eyes upon him, that he meant nothing to me. How could the nights of debauchery I spent with Nicolas and Warin mean aught to me when compared with the love that you and I share? Treachery and trickery, 'twas the game both of them played."

Unbending from the rigid posture he had assumed, Dafydd bowed his head and murmured, "'Tis truth, my king, that 'tis difficult to hear, painful to think on, and yet 'tis also truth that 'tis better for having it in the open betwixt us."

"Dafydd, cariad." Christopher moved so that he knelt in front of Dafydd, held his face between his hands, met him eye to eye. "I love you with all that I am. A deep, abiding love that transcends anything I have felt before. You are my soul, my heart. I would never speak of this again after today, I but needed to say it now, and it is my hope that you understand."

After a long moment of gazing deep into each other's eyes, Dafydd leaned closer. "Aye," he said softly. "'Tis well."

They stayed on the beach long after that, watching the waves, sharing their warmth beneath the cloak. Silently each girded himself for the night ahead, as even though they did not say it in words, both knew there was one more barrier to cross.

[21]
A Brutal Truth

WHEN the sun began to lower in the sky, Christopher and Dafydd made their way across the beach, back toward the village. The inn was empty, as the innkeeper had determined that privacy was important for his guest. He served them a meal in the common room, and it was clear he had received provisions from Godfrey's keep. The stew was much better than what they had been served the previous night, as was the wine.

The innkeeper's son bowed his way into the room to report that he had passed the message on to Sir Godfrey and Alain in turn, and that Christopher's men had arrived from Sir Mortimer's keep. Smiling his thanks, Christopher gifted the lad with a few copper coins.

Once they had finished the meal, Christopher picked up the flagon of wine, and he and Dafydd retreated up the stairs. They found that the room had been freshened in their absence, and a fire burned brightly in the hearth. Although they were the only guests at the inn, Dafydd bolted the door.

When he turned, Christopher pulled him into a tight embrace. "'Tis cold, cariad. I would feel your skin pressed against mine beneath the furs."

"Aye," Dafydd said, and he reached up to caress the side of Christopher's face. "In truth I would feel more than that."

Christopher turned to press his lips into Dafydd's palm and murmured, "Then you must needs undress."

They stepped back reluctantly from each other's warmth, turned to disrobe, and then settled on the pallet under the mound of furs. Lying facing one another, they refrained from touching with more than their gaze. Desire coursed through both of them. Dafydd opened his mouth and issued a small moan.

Only then did Christopher move forward, urge Dafydd to roll onto his back, and settle atop him. Although he did not speak again, his true feelings were communicated through the gentleness of his touch. He pressed kisses upon Dafydd's fluttering eyelids and kissed the tip of his nose. He teased against the seam of Dafydd's lips with his tongue and nibbled the scruff on his cheeks.

Dafydd swelled up against Christopher's body and looped his arms tightly around him. He spread his legs wider, allowing Christopher to settle in closer against his warmth.

They moved in a manner they were long accustomed to, fingers and mouths exploring, eliciting moans of need and shudders of pleasure. At last, Christopher rose up, the furs skimming down his back. He trailed a hand down Dafydd's thigh, and Dafydd complied by raising his leg. He gazed up at the king through eyes narrowed with desire. Christopher bent down and claimed another sweet kiss as he reached for the pot of cream.

The chill of the room was chased away by the warmth of the love between them. Christopher continued to watch Dafydd as he fingered him gently, and Dafydd's member stiffened further under the observation. Dafydd rose up on one elbow and reached down to cup his sack against his body that he might watch Christopher's fingers as they disappeared inside his passage. Propped up this way, Christopher was given access to kiss the top of Dafydd's head as he held his fingers deep inside.

Approaching the zenith, Dafydd lowered back to the furs and raised both legs, holding them tightly up against his chest. Christopher extracted his fingers and pressed the head of his cock against Dafydd's entrance.

Once Christopher sank inside, Dafydd released his hold on his legs and reached up to cup his hands behind Christopher's head. He held Christopher in place long enough to make eye contact, and then he lowered his hands to Christopher's shoulders and closed his own eyes.

With one hand braced on the pallet beside Dafydd's head, Christopher reached between their bodies and closed his other hand around Dafydd's cock. He held inside Dafydd as he stroked him and listened to Dafydd's hitched breathing. When Dafydd's muscles began to twitch, Christopher began to move inside him.

Dafydd tightened his grip on Christopher's shoulders, and that was Christopher's cue to thrust harder. Opening his mouth for one small moan, Dafydd curled up so that his cheek touched Christopher's just as he came.

Turning to brush his lips against Dafydd's cheek, Christopher then began to thrust harder. It wasn't long before he joined Dafydd in release.

After a moment, Christopher slipped out of Dafydd's passage and spooned against him.

With the furs bunched around their waists, they allowed the tremors to leave their bodies, and then Christopher sat up and poured a goblet of wine. After taking a healthy swallow, he offered it to Dafydd. Dafydd shook his head and rolled to lie on his belly, his cheek pillowed on crossed arms as he gazed into the fire.

Christopher remained sitting behind him, savoring the wine as he looked upon Dafydd's back. The flickering firelight played over the series of raised welts that webbed Dafydd's skin, causing eerie shadows. At last, he set his goblet aside, took a deep breath, and reached out to lay a fingertip against one of the scars. Unbidden, the memory of the day he spent in the dungeons at Strasnedh, with Simon recounting the tortuous lashings Dafydd had endured, entered his mind.

Dafydd flinched but remained where he was as he felt Christopher's finger trace the length of the scar. It was a deliberate move, touching the scar. It was rare that Christopher did it, and after the recent talk of Warin, Dafydd suspected this action would initiate some deeper conversation between them. While he knew this talk was long overdue, it still troubled him to share it, even with his lover.

"Tell me of it, Dafydd," Christopher said his voice thick with emotion.

"I have. And you have seen, by your own admission," Dafydd said.

Christopher bent down and pressed a kiss on the track his finger had traced on Dafydd's back. When he sat up he said, "'Tis the last barrier betwixt us, Dafydd, the wedge, as we have called it. Aye, Simon described it, leaving little to my imagination, and you have recounted the parts you think me capable of hearing, but we must needs bring it all out into the open, lest it fester and lead to another rift. In any case, as you said to me earlier when we spoke of my past with Nicolas and Warin, 'tis best to have no lingering secrets betwixt us."

Dafydd covered his face with his arm and was silent.

After a moment, Christopher resumed tracing each scar with a gentle finger. When the silence was broken, Dafydd's voice was muffled.

"Warin kept me prisoner; that much you know. His guards stripped me of my clothing, and thus my dignity, on the first day of my imprisonment. Each time he visited me, I defied him, and that angered him all the more." Dafydd moved his arm away from his face but did not turn to look at Christopher as he continued. "You know the man. You know what he is capable of. What purpose does it serve to have me tell you the vile things he did to my body?"

"The purpose," Christopher said, resting his hand on Dafydd's hip, "is that if you do not, it will grow inside you. Yes, in truth, I know he flogged you, I know you resisted, and I know he told you 'twas me he wished to destroy. But what I do not understand is your fear. I have told you he will not return, and you are safe whenever you are with me, as I would strike him down in his tracks were he to threaten you again." He paused and then leaned closer that he might speak softly into Dafydd's ear. "I would that you tell me the worst of it, as 'tis my belief that is the root of your fear."

"I came here, Christopher, I ventured all this way on my own, that I might show you I can master my fear," Dafydd said.

"Aye," Christopher said. "And yet I would have you share this memory, that we might leave it behind in this place, where 'tis likely we will not visit again, and that we might return to Lysnowydh and make a new beginning."

Moving onto his side and drawing his knees up against his body in a protective way, Dafydd said, "'Twas wrong, Christopher, that Warin took such delight in beating me with his whip. It angered him that I would not cry out with the incredible pain. Sometimes he lost whatever small amount of control he had whilst the others watched, but 'twas worse when he sent them from the room, leaving only me to witness and experience his pique."

Christopher moved to sit on the hearth in front of Dafydd, that he might watch the shifting emotions on his lover's face as he spoke, even though Dafydd kept his eyes averted.

"Ten lashes, and then they released the bonds. As time went on, e'en though I never cried out with the pain, I lost the ability to remain on my feet once I was released. When Warin was not able to contain his anger until the guards left, he pissed on my back and rained curses upon me. The first time, when he saw how it affected me, he crowed and made it a regular part of the torture." Dafydd shifted his eyes to Christopher's face, "You must needs brace, Christopher, as that was by far not the worst of it."

"Aye, I expected it was not," Christopher said, his face ashen, his hand clenched in a fist.

"One night before the end, when Warin came, 'twas clear he had overindulged in wine. He directed his guards to bind my hands to the wall, and then he bid them leave. 'Twas rare, as he usually wanted witness to his brutality. I leaned my head against the wall and closed my eyes as I listened to him prepare, and I knew he had disrobed. His cock, when I opened my eyes once, was engorged. The whip dangled from his hand."

At this point in the retelling, Dafydd closed his eyes as he went back deep inside himself to reveal this memory.

"This time, there were more than ten lashes. Fifteen, as I counted when he did not. I was weak, but I drew blood biting my lip to keep from crying out. I heard him throw the whip across the room in disgust, and then he came and pushed himself against my back, his breath sour with wine as told me things would be different this night. He released my hands from the manacles, but caught me tight against him so I would not drop to the floor."

Christopher watched as Dafydd attempted to repress a shudder, but he remained on the hearth, giving Dafydd his space to retell the story.

Dafydd opened his eyes. Christopher was unprepared for the pain that etched across Dafydd's face. "He dropped me in the center of the room. I lacked the strength to move away from him, but it was no matter, as there was nowhere for me to go. Though I was expecting that eventually he would violate me, I was not ready for the incredible pain, and I cried out."

As Dafydd paused to catch his breath, Christopher clenched his hand into a fist.

"The first time did not last long, but he made it a part of his torture from that point on. Each time 'twas the same, he entered the room with his guards, and bid them leave once they chained me to the wall. When the lashing was complete, he released me and fucked me. Still I did not break, and did not cry out again after the first time. I believe he despaired of ever breaking me."

Unable to hold back, Christopher spoke, his voice breaking on the words, "Might I hold you, Dafydd?"

In answer, Dafydd shifted back on the pallet and held his arms open. Christopher slipped down in front of him, facing him to maintain eye contact.

"The fear, Christopher, comes from the knowledge that he but used me to seek some revenge I do not understand, revenge against you. Whilst he rammed his cock into me so hard that my knees scraped against the floor, he said he meant to ruin me so that you would not want me any longer."

Although he allowed Christopher to touch him, Dafydd held himself rigid. He closed his eyes before he continued.

"The last time, I was so weakened by his abuse of my body that I was unable to stand. 'Twas only when the whip touched me that I was able to force myself to my feet. I saw cold anger in his eyes, and I feared he meant deeper harm, mayhap even to kill me." Suppressing another shudder and dropping his voice to a whisper, Dafydd said, "That was the night he asked me what you called me whilst we were in bed. I have told you that part before, and now 'tis set in its proper context. 'Twas that night when he finally, truly, broke me."

Christopher eased closer and tucked his head under Dafydd's chin, against the hollow of his throat. He wrapped his arm tightly around Dafydd's back and pulled him as close as he was able. "I can take none of that away, Dafydd. What is done, is done. Forevermore, 'tis a part of your being, and through the recounting, 'tis now also a part of my being. Would that I could remove it. Would that I could say the right words," he drew a ragged breath.

Only then did Dafydd release the tight hold on his body, relax into Christopher's embrace, and move to wrap an arm around Christopher's back.

"Do not let him win, Dafydd," Christopher said.

Completely spent, Dafydd did not respond. He opened his hand and placed it against Christopher's back, holding him close.

The fire burned down to embers in the hearth, and eventually both drifted to sleep.

❦ 22 ❦
Tenderness in the Aftermath

WHEN Christopher woke the next morning, he found he was alone. Dafydd rising from their nest that had triggered his awakening. He found that Dafydd stood by the window, massive in his nakedness, seemingly unaware of the cold in the room. Shivering, Christopher rose from the pallet and went to stand behind him, close but not touching.

"I must needs go below stairs," Christopher murmured, "to request a tub and hot water for your bath."

Startled from his reverie, Dafydd turned. Even in the soft light of dawn, his eyes were shadowed, and it was difficult to see into their depths. "Nay, my king. I will go below and ask for water and a tub if you wish it. 'Tis my duty to provide for you in this case."

Christopher could sense that Dafydd needed space, so he backed away. "Nay, there is no duty here beyond the simple fact that we both need the soothing waters of a bath. Dress, tend the fire, and I will return anon." He smiled to soften his words, turned, and began to pull on his clothing.

With his back turned, Christopher did not see Dafydd raise his hand, did not see the longing that overtook his features for a moment before he dropped his hand and murmured, "As you wish."

Once dressed, Christopher turned back, the corners of his mouth lifted in the barest suggestion of a smile as he said, "I shall not be long."

Christopher hurried down the stairs. Although he sensed that Dafydd needed time to adjust to the fact that Christopher now knew the details of Warin's torture, he did not want to leave him for too long. He knew that he also needed time to come to terms with the maelstrom of emotions each of them had unleashed. In this primitive place, he was not sure a tub could be had, but he would ask, as he felt some semblance of normalcy would benefit them both.

He found the innkeeper idling in the common room.

"I have need of a tub," Christopher said by way of greeting, "and water to fill it. We also require food for breaking our fast."

"Aye, your majesty," said the man, standing at attention. "Would you prefer I send to the keep? The tub we possess in the inn is small, housed at present in the stable. Mayhap if I send my boy up to the keep, he can return not only with a more suitable vessel but your body servant as well."

"Nay, there is not time," Christopher said. "E'en if 'tis small, I am quite sure your tub will suffice. In any case, we have no need for either of our servants when we have each other."

"Aye, your majesty," the innkeeper said with a deep bow. "Let me have my son bring the tub in that you might examine it. In the meantime I shall begin to heat the water. 'Twill take many trips to deliver it above stairs, but it shall be done."

"My thanks," Christopher said. He cocked his head to the side. "How is it that you still have no other occupants here at the inn? How is it that half the village is not here gossiping at the strange requests, not to mention the presence of your king?"

"Begging your pardon, majesty," the innkeeper said with another bow. "'Twas not my intention to have any to intrude upon your privacy, and gossiping is best left to women sorting fish."

"'Tis well," Christopher said as he perched on a stool by the fireside. "'Tis not my intention that Sir Dafydd and I stay here for much longer, mayhap a day or two more. When I leave, I grant you right of renaming your establishment 'The King's Arms.' You have served me well."

"Oh, your majesty," the innkeeper said, his face glowing red with pleasure. "'Tis a right grand gift you bestow."

"Rightfully earned," Christopher said.

Nibbling on the cheese and bread the innkeeper's son laid before him, Christopher watched as the tub was dragged into the room and scrubbed before the blazing main hearth. In truth it was not fit to hold either of them, but it would serve its purpose. A great cauldron of water was set over the hearth, and the innkeeper's son told Christopher shyly that another one bubbled in the kitchen. Before long, all was ready.

Meanwhile, above stairs, Dafydd dressed and then bent to attend to the fire. He adjusted the log in the grate and blew upon the embers until tiny flames licked around the wood. When the fire seemed to catch, he returned to the window and resumed his study of the ocean. His thoughts swirled around not only the retelling he had provided the night before, but also the words that had passed between himself and Christopher in the past few days.

All things taken under consideration, he knew that the simple act of journeying this far had done much to dispel the memory of his captivity with Warin. There had been no need to relive the horrors as he had, and yet tickling somewhere deep within him was the knowledge that, by revealing all to Christopher, he had given over some of the revulsion. He knew beyond the shadow of a doubt that Christopher longed for Dafydd's healing and longed for things to be as they once were. Christopher had said that he could not take away any of the horror that Dafydd had shared, but he was not certain it was so. In sharing the nightmare more completely than he yet had, he himself felt a lightening of the burden.

Soon Dafydd heard the heavy tread on the stair and knew it signaled the arrival of the tub, water, victuals, and the king. He wanted no awkwardness between them, so he set his mind that, once the bathing was through, there would be another difficult conversation between them.

As the innkeeper and his son brought in the tub and began carrying in buckets of warm water to fill it, Dafydd considered the many proofs of Christopher's love: The firm hand that had guided him in his early days of becoming the king's marshal. The subtle ways Christopher had let him prove his worth to the men, particularly in dealing with the first cattle raid. Dafydd had disagreed with Christopher in front of the men about how best to deal with the raid, but it had proven that Dafydd had the best interests of Lysnowydh and its king at heart, where the others thought only to forward their own interests.

The first in a chain of buckets was dumped into the tub by the innkeeper and his son, and Dafydd continued the litany of Christopher's caring in his head. There the infinite care bestowed upon him when he was first returned from Strasnedh. Dafydd recalled the night Christopher had rekindled the physical relationship between them in his cottage, and although a fair amount of pain had accompanied that joining, Christopher had been patient and loving.

Dafydd reflected that Christopher was a hard man, a king through and through, and the epiphany visited him that, in spite of the hardness of the man who loved him, he was able to show softness, but only to Dafydd. Tears filled his eyes and emotion clogged his throat, but he held himself in check.

Christopher brought the last bucket of water, and the innkeeper departed with his son. After testing the water, and deeming it was perfect in temperature, Christopher turned to face Dafydd. He gestured that Dafydd should disrobe and get in the tub.

"Nay, Christopher," Dafydd said. Only a small tremor betrayed the emotion he strove to keep in check. "You must needs bathe first."

"No disobedience, cariad," Christopher said firmly. "If there is any warmth left when you have finished, I shall take my turn. You must needs—" And only here did he display any of the feelings he might have, as soft color crept across his cheeks and he continued in a softer voice, "As I said last night, I cannot remove the pain that lingers in your being from the captivity and torture you suffered at Warin's hands. Yet I try now, in some small and mayhap pathetic way, to make things right."

With one small shiver, Dafydd turned and began to remove his clothing. He kept his back presented to Christopher as he stripped off his shirt and chausses. It had been many weeks since last he had bathed, and he sighed in pleasure as he sank into the warmth of the tub. Even though it was too small, and his knees protruded as he was nearly bent in half, the heat of the water settled through all of him. When he opened his eyes, he found Christopher seated on the hearth, watching him.

"Would you let me bathe you?" Christopher asked.

"Aye," Dafydd said. "Of course. You are no stranger to the task."

"'Tis true," Christopher said as he moved forward and picked up a cloth, "and yet I thought you might crave the solitude."

"Nay," Dafydd said, and his body trembled when Christopher began to drag the soaped cloth over his back. "I crave your touch, my king."

Christopher soaped the cloth again and shifted to wash the front of Dafydd's body. He kept his head bowed, his eyes averted from Dafydd's. "I am sorry I coaxed you to tell me the story last night, Dafydd. Mayhap 'twas best left unsaid."

"Do not be sorry," Dafydd whispered.

"Dafydd," Christopher said as his hand stilled, "I but told you once that betimes anger and passion are entwined." He raised his head at last to meet Dafydd's gaze. "In battle I am as fierce as the lion that ramps upon my shield. I fear nothing, and I relish the fight. Affairs of the heart are quite another thing. Betimes I—" He faltered, then took a deep breath and continued. "You said you felt fear, and know that I feel helpless. I wish to remove all the hurt from you, I wish to make you whole. Mayhap I wish to pretend none of it ever happened." He dropped the cloth into the water and reached up to press his thumb against Dafydd's lower lip. "I love you, Dafydd, with all of my heart and all of my soul. I love you with a body that ofttimes betrays me."

Although Dafydd had struggled with his emotions, this honest talk cut deeper than the revelations of the night before. He reached up and cupped his wet hand over Christopher's as a tear dripped down his cheek. "I understand," he said simply.

Christopher bent forward and pressed his lips against Dafydd's, and in that simple kiss, they made their peace.

Clearing his throat, Christopher sat back. "Does it help, being clean again?"

"What helps," Dafydd said, "is the words you say. Aye, the warm water soothes, but 'tis the balm of your love that heals." He leaned his back against the edge of the tub, relaxing as much as he was able in the cramped space.

Christopher smiled as he wrung the water from the cloth and spread it over the edge of the tub. "'Tis said that love is the great healer."

"Aye," Dafydd said, and with an effort he levered himself up and out of the tub. "My thanks for allowing me the tub first, my king, and now you must needs wash. I would take one last walk upon the beach before we return home."

Christopher undressed quickly and then settled into the small tub. "I would keep you here yet another night, cariad. I would trade ugly memories for pleasant ones ere we must needs depart for Lysnowydh."

"'Tis well," Dafydd said. Once he had dressed, he knelt beside the tub that he might help Christopher complete his bath.

❧ 23 ❧
Promises Made

ONCE the bathing was complete and their fast had been broken, Christopher and Dafydd descended the stairs and made their way out into the hazy sun of midmorning. The string of storms that had unleashed their fury on the rocky coastline had passed, and though there was still a chill in the air, the sun lent an illusion of warmth.

In an attempt to blend into their surroundings, both men were dressed in old and worn clothing. Christopher carried himself like a king, and thus the illusion was lost on most. The townsfolk were simple, yet they did not take lightly the honor of their king sheltering with them. Aside from the gawking stares, king and woodsman were left to go about their business unmolested.

"There is a shop in town where we can buy some bread and, if we are lucky, a bit of cheese," Dafydd said as they walked through the town.

"'Tis well," Christopher said. "'Tis my desire to walk until the sun sinks low in the sky, does that suit you?"

"Aye," Dafydd said.

The inn was at one end of the village, and the shop with the bread was at the other end. Dafydd said he would go in to buy what was needed; Christopher said he would wait as he had no wish to make the shopkeeper uncomfortable.

Christopher lounged against a stile as he waited. He watched seagulls wheeling over the flotsam on the beach. He longed for home, wondered how Lysnowydh fared while he was away, but he was determined to leave a pleasant memory in place of the ugliness that had been dredged up the previous night. He hoped they could leave the agony of Warin in this distant location, and wanted to ensure pleasant memories would blot out the pain.

After Dafydd emerged from the shop, the two men set out across the expanse of beach until they reached the rocky edge of the shore. There they picked their way along in silence, each lost in his own thoughts and memories.

Once they rounded the promontory at the far end of the natural inlet, they came to a place where forward progress would be difficult, so they decided to stop for their meal. After searching for a sandy spot, they settled, their backs against a rock.

Dafydd took a loaf of barley bread from the oiled cloth in which it had been wrapped. He broke off a hunk of bread and a hunk from the wedge of cheese, and handed both over with a rueful smile. "The merchant did not have any wine, but he did give me a skin of water."

The fresh air and the morning's exercise had given them both a hearty appetite. They had passed their trek in silence and were loath to break the silence as they ate.

Christopher made quick work of his bread and then licked his fingers. He slouched back against the rock, hands folded behind his head, as he looked up into the faded blue sky. Once Dafydd had finished his meal, Christopher reached over absently for Dafydd's hand and kissed the back of it.

"We must needs start for home soon," Christopher said.

"Aye," Dafydd replied. "I thought to spend a day with Sir Godfrey to mollify any slight he might feel that we traveled all this way and then ignored his hospitality."

"'Tis wise," Christopher said. "And 'tis much the same as I thought." His hand still twined with Dafydd's, he squeezed gently and said, "We must needs speak of the future ere we depart for home."

"My king?" Dafydd said, a frown collecting on his brow.

Christopher sighed and turned to meet Dafydd's gaze. "The future, Dafydd, our future. Aye, 'tis certain that the bond betwixt us is strong, mayhap stronger than e'er it was, and yet I ask you what you desire once we return to Lysnowydh keep."

Knowing it was the last barrier between them, Dafydd dipped his head. In his heart, he knew what he wanted, yet he was unsure how the warrior king would accept it. Slowly he disentangled his hand from Christopher's and said, "I crave the serenity of my stillroom."

"Forevermore? You have no wish to reassume your position as marshal?" Christopher asked. "You possess the physical strength, Dafydd. And the mental strength returns more each day."

"Aye," Dafydd said slowly. "And yet it has never been my way to be warlike."

Christopher propped his chin in his hand and gazed across the rocks toward where the waves sent spray into the air. A silence fell between them for a time, broken only by the cries of the gulls as they dove toward the water.

"Mayhap," Christopher said at last, "'tis not your way to be warlike, yet when the need arises, you possess the skill."

"When it comes to defending you, my king, or Anwyll, or Lysnowydh, aye, I possess the skill and the desire."

"Then we must needs strike a bargain betwixt us, cariad," Christopher said, moving closer that he and Dafydd were eye to eye. "I will grant you the peace of your stillroom, and you will cast your might behind mine own should the need arise."

"There need be no bargain," Dafydd said. "When the time comes that an army is needed, you know full well I shall be ready." He hunched in on himself and turned his face away from the king's.

"What troubles you, Dafydd?" Christopher asked, his voice gentle with concern, not harsh with command.

"'Tis naught," Dafydd said.

"'Tis a lie," Christopher said. "I see the weighty thoughts that tumble through your mind."

"You are demanding," Dafydd said, "both in this need to know my thoughts and in the casting of bargains between us."

"Peace, Dafydd," Christopher said, and he settled closer, laid an arm over Dafydd's shoulders, and pulled him close. "Mayhap the choosing of words was poor. In truth, 'tis my fervent desire that we be yoked, side by side, in the daily business of Lysnowydh. It pains me that you have been absent from my side in the drilling of troops, in the strategizing of our defenses, in many aspects of our daily lives. I but sought to return us to what we had before, and mayhap 'tis not possible, mayhap 'tis still too soon."

Dafydd sighed and relaxed against Christopher's body. He was quiet for a while, and when he finally spoke, his voice was soft against the backdrop of the pounding surf behind them. "My apologies."

"Nay, cariad," Christopher said, and he bent close to press a kiss upon Dafydd's brow. "In time the change will come. And whether it be you resuming your role, or me changing my views, together we are one."

There was a chill in the breeze that eddied around them, and with one final kiss, Christopher stood and held his hand down to Dafydd. "Come, let us begin the walk back ere the cold settles into our bones."

Hand in hand, they began their walk back. It was difficult going, and in places they had to release their hold on one another, but eventually they walked again upon the smooth sandy shore. Before they reached the road leading into the village, Dafydd pulled back on Christopher's hand, halting their progress.

"My king," he said softly, "much progress has been made o'er these past few days. I have begun along the road to full healing. Let not this one conversation cast a dark cloud upon the things we have accomplished. I will not vow that I will never come forth from my stillroom to stand again as marshal to your troops, and yet I will not vow that I will. What I will vow is my love, my strength, and my support. I will vow that I will shed the evil memories and I will find my way from the darkness."

"And I will vow," Christopher said, "to love you always and give you the space that you need. I vow my protection, but more, I vow my understanding."

After pulling Christopher close for just a bare moment that the vows might be sealed with a human touch between them, Dafydd stepped back and said, "'Tis well."

The shadows were long as they made their way through the small village, back to the inn. The innkeeper once again provided a meal and privacy in the common room for them to devour it. When the meal was done, Christopher reached for Dafydd's hand.

"Come, cariad," Christopher said. "Tomorrow we shall depart for Sir Godfrey's keep, and soon we shall begin our lives afresh."

Dafydd stood and tucked his hand inside Christopher's.

"Tonight we shall spend one last night here and block out whatever lingering ugliness remains," Christopher said as he led Dafydd toward the stairs.

"'Tis blocked, my king," Dafydd murmured.

"Mayhap in your mind," Christopher said, "yet 'tis not fully blocked in mine."

❦⟨24⟩❦
Memories Traded

UPSTAIRS, a branch of candles lent a soft warmth to the shabby room. The pallet had been replaced before the blazing hearth after the tub was removed, and the furs freshened and fluffed. Christopher removed his cloak and laid it across the bedframe, then went to sit in one of the chairs.

After bolting the door, Dafydd came to kneel before Christopher and began working on the lacings of his boots.

"Though 'tis early, I would to bed," Christopher said. He laid a gentle hand on Dafydd's shoulder.

When he had removed both of the king's boots, Dafydd sat back on his heels and looked up. "As would I." He did not move from his position.

"What is it?" Christopher said.

"Last night…" Dafydd spoke slowly, and even though his face was in shadow, it was clear that soft color crept across his cheeks.

Christopher moved from the chair and knelt on the floor beside Dafydd. He did not urge him to continue with words but just reached for Dafydd's hand and held it.

"I have been thinking on your words, my king. You said I must not let him win."

Christopher nodded, knowing those were the last whispered words he said to Dafydd the previous night, before they drifted into an uneasy sleep filled with nightmares brought about by Dafydd's awful tale of Warin.

"I will not," Dafydd said as he reached for Christopher's hand.

"'Tis well," Christopher said, and he leaned closer to seal the promise with a kiss.

Together they rose and undressed. Christopher bent to rearrange the furs on the pallet, then stood to blow out the candles. Dafydd put another log on the fire and settled on the pallet first, his back resting against the foot of the bed, his long legs splayed wide. Desire washed through him slowly and his cock stiffened.

When Christopher turned from his task, it was evident that desire coursed through him as well. He looked down at Dafydd and said, "I would hold you, cariad."

Shifting forward, Dafydd allowed Christopher to settle behind him and cradle him between his strong legs. Dafydd turned and murmured against Christopher's cheek, "Gwnei 'm balfalu da."

Trailing his fingers down the center of Dafydd's chest, Christopher moved close enough that his golden hair fell forward over Dafydd's shoulder. "Tell me the words of your heart," he murmured.

"You know the words, my king. I but told you that you make me feel good." Dafydd rested his hands against Christopher's legs where they framed his body.

"Beunydd," Christopher whispered. He teased his fingers against the base of Dafydd's erection and then lower to cup his balls. "You are alive, cariad, and strong." He squeezed gently. "And mine."

"Ond eiddo," Dafydd said, "anwylyd."

Releasing his hold, Christopher once again trailed his fingers over Dafydd's skin and teased over his nipples before withdrawing his hand to reach for the pot of cream. He bent forward to nibble at the spot where neck met shoulder as he lowered his slick fingers back down to encircle Dafydd's cock.

Through narrowed eyes, Dafydd watched Christopher's hand upon his cock, watched as the firelight danced over the slick trail. He became lost in a world of sensation as Christopher continued to stroke his cock and nibble at his neck. Through parted lips, he moaned, and eventually his eyes slipped closed.

Moving his lips from Dafydd's neck, Christopher whispered, "Let go, Dafydd."

Arching against the tight grip on his cock and the tickling whisper in his ear, Dafydd tightened his hands on Christopher's legs. He groaned again when Christopher released him long enough to reach for more cream, and then the groan caught in his throat when the stroking was renewed.

As his climax neared, Dafydd turned his head and pressed against Christopher's cheek. He opened his mouth but was unable to form words as he came. He bucked up against Christopher's hand and was held firmly as tremors chased through his body. He allowed himself to sink into the warmth of being held this way as he struggled to catch his breath.

Slowly, Christopher released his hold and pressed his hand flat against Dafydd's belly. "I love you, cariad," he whispered. "Beunydd." He massaged a small circle against Dafydd's flesh, rubbing the rest of the cream and Dafydd's issue into his skin.

A log cracked in the fire, and outside the wind picked up as another storm began to roll in. Dafydd stirred and turned against Christopher's body, so that when Christopher bent his head down, their lips touched. The kiss deepened, and Dafydd reached up to tuck his hand around Christopher's neck, holding him close.

When they broke apart, breathless from the intensity, Dafydd whispered, "If I give you my thanks, you will tell me 'tis not necessary. But know this, my king: all that has passed between us here makes me stronger and able to face whatever challenges are still ahead. Your love gives me strength; your passion makes me whole. Your desire fuels mine own. 'Rwy'n dy garu di."

Christopher slid his arm behind Dafydd's back and held him close. "You possessed the strength already, cariad. Mayhap 'tis just that our stay here has cleared your mind. I will accept your thanks, as I know they are given from your heart. You have power in abundance, Dafydd; I still shiver at the force of it."

Twisting so that he was on his knees, Dafydd reached up and cupped the sides of Christopher's face between his hands. "The power has always been there, aye. 'Tis restored by your touch." He bent forward for a kiss and then moved back, trailing his hands across Christopher's arms, down to rest on his hips. "I would taste you."

Drawing in his breath, Christopher nodded and then lay back against the furs. He pulled his knees up and let his legs fall open. In truth, touching Dafydd's body and bringing him to release had enflamed him. His cock twitched when Dafydd dipped and ran his tongue over the head.

Lying flat on his belly, Dafydd wrapped one arm around Christopher's leg and eased in close. He continued with the teasing, circled the head of Christopher's cock, pushed the point of his tongue into the slit, and coaxed forth a taste of his lover's essence.

Christopher settled back further against the furs and moaned at the dual sensation of their warmth below him and Dafydd's clever mouth above him. He unclenched one hand and reached up to grip Dafydd's hair. Arching his neck back, he opened his mouth and groaned.

The storm that brewed outside was gentler than the previous storms that had unleashed their fury against the rugged coastline. Wind buffeted the small inn and matched the growing passion inside.

When Christopher murmured the word *please*, Dafydd ceased with the teasing, opened his mouth, and swallowed him down to the base of his throbbing cock. He hummed low in his throat and felt the tremors chase through Christopher's body. As he pulled up, he stole a glance and saw that Christopher was lost in the world of sensation. This time as he sank down again, he grazed with his teeth, and Christopher released the hold on his hair and fell back with arms stretched wide.

Dafydd allowed himself a moment to take in the sight of Christopher sprawled against the furs, every bit as powerful as before, but vulnerable to the hold that Dafydd had over him in that moment. It clicked then, in Dafydd's mind, that he did indeed still possess the power that Christopher had said. One misstep into hell had not changed everything.

With that knowledge, Dafydd resumed his gentle attack on Christopher's body, increasing the fervor as he tightened his lips and bobbed his head faster. He curled both hands up around Christopher's hips, anchoring him in reality. Dafydd felt the pulsing through Christopher's cock, and judged by the labored sounds of his breathing the moment when climax overtook him. Tightening his lips, he swallowed all.

When Christopher relaxed down against the furs, utterly spent, Dafydd eased up, releasing him with a soft pop. He moved up so that their bodies twined together side by side, one large hand possessively on Christopher's hip. Together they listened to the wind blowing rain against the window, until at last Christopher shivered. Although it was more from the expense of emotion, Dafydd still reached to draw the furs up over their bodies.

"Mayhap I should add yet another log to the fire," he murmured.

"Not yet awhile," Christopher said, his voice thick. "I would feel you against me, hold you as you hold me."

"Aye," Dafydd said as he eased closer to press a soft kiss on Christopher's cheek.

They were silent then, communicating only with the feel of skin pressed against skin.

❧{25}❧
Journey Home

THE sky was gray the next morning, but the wind and rain had eased. Dafydd woke first and coaxed the fire to life while Christopher stirred awake behind him. Looking back over his shoulder, Dafydd smiled at the glimpses of Christopher's flesh amongst the furs.

"Were we not expected at Sir Godfrey's keep this morn, I would of necessity take advantage of you, my king," he murmured.

Eyelids fluttering, Christopher spoke, his voice hoarse with sleep. "Would that I could let you, yet I find deep in my soul that I am anxious to return home."

"Home," Dafydd said. "Aye, the need for home is strong within me as well."

The water in the basin was cold, yet they splashed it on their faces and then stood to pull on their clothing. The fire warmed them. When they were dressed, they left the room together and descended the stairs.

"Your majesty," the innkeeper greeted them. "I have sent my son to the keep, as 'twas my understanding you wished for your servants this day."

"Aye, 'tis truth," Christopher said. He and Dafydd settled on stools at the table in the common room. "Although we are loath to leave the comfort we find here, we must needs begin our journey home soon."

The innkeeper bowed. "I truly cannot express my gratitude that you have chosen to spend as much time in my humble inn as you have. 'Tis truly an honor."

Christopher smiled by way of answer, and when the oat stirrabout was set before them, he attacked it with gusto. Beside him, Dafydd had an equal appetite. When they had finished eating, they took up their tankards of ale and waited for the return of Alain and John.

"I am certain," Christopher said, "that Sir Godfrey will provide a bath and mayhap his solar for our use."

"I seem to recall that the first time we came to his keep, Sir Godfrey's wife attended your bath, and his daughter shyly attended mine," Dafydd said as he set his tankard aside.

Turning to study Dafydd's profile, Christopher said, "Aye, 'tis truth. Methinks this time he will grant us ourselves, and privacy."

"Mayhap," Dafydd said.

Before long they heard the sound of horses outside, and soon after, Alain and John joined them. Smiles wreathed both their faces.

Dafydd slipped from the stool and said, "I would speak with John."

"Of course," Christopher said. "Go above with him whilst he gathers our things."

Dafydd led the way, and John fell into step behind him. Christopher turned to find Alain waiting by the front door. He beckoned as he turned on the stool.

"How do the men fare?" Christopher asked as Alain approached.

"Well, your majesty," Alain said as he bowed. "They have folded in with Sir Godfrey's men. They run patrols and drill with them."

"'Tis well," Christopher said. He glanced over his shoulder and then stood, moving closer to Alain that he might speak in confidence. "I know you would not ask, but know that things are well betwixt Dafydd and me."

"Aye, your majesty," Alain murmured. "I had no doubt 'twould be the case."

With a smile, Christopher stepped back. He picked up his tankard and drained the rest. "Pay the innkeeper here well; I would wait outside."

Above stairs, the conversation was more intimate. From the first day Dafydd had found himself set to live in the mighty keep at Lysnowydh, he had had difficulty accepting the fact that he did, in fact, require the services of a body servant. In the end, his relationship with John had become a friendly one; they were not merely master and servant.

"You need not say it, Dafydd," John said as he reached for Dafydd's hand. "I see with mine own eyes that your journey has had the effect you desired."

"Aye," Dafydd said as he squeezed and then released John's hand. "'Twas as I expected, and yet 'twas more than I expected. King Christopher is many things. He is brutal, yet there resides within him a wealth of love. Although betimes his actions seem harsh, I see and understand the reasons for them. Many would not; many would damn him for the things he does." Dafydd said.

John was silent for a moment and then said, "I have seen King Christopher's fervor firsthand many times, Dafydd. He is king, and as such he must needs be hard."

"'Tis well," Dafydd said.

John began to gather the personal items that belonged to the king and Dafydd. He wrapped them into a tight bundle.

ONCE the bundle was packed and the room was set to rights, Dafydd and John joined Alain below in the common room. The innkeeper had already been paid, so the threesome joined Christopher, and together they left the small village and picked their way up the rocky path toward the keep on the hillside.

The gates stood open, as Christopher and Dafydd were expected. Sir Godfrey waited for them in the bailey and greeted King Christopher as though the visit was not out of the ordinary.

"I welcome you, my liege," Sir Godfrey said as he bowed. "I know, of a necessity, that your visit will be short. My lady and I have vacated our solar that you and Sir Dafydd might bathe and sleep in privacy this night. 'Twould be an honor if you would share the evening meal in the hall this eve, but if you desire to sup in your room, 'twill be arranged."

Christopher dismounted and handed his reins to a waiting stable boy. He turned and watched Dafydd dismount before he said, "You are a good man, Godfrey. Though 'tis midday, Dafydd and I will gladly take advantage of the bath, and we will join you in the hall for dinner anon. 'Tis truth, we cannot stay past the morrow, but thank you for this hospitality."

"Come inside; wait by the hearth as the bath is prepared," Sir Godfrey said. "Would you wish for two baths and the assistance of my lady and daughter?"

"Nay, one will suffice," Christopher said with a smile.

"'Tis well," Sir Godfrey said.

When they entered the keep, Christopher and Dafydd went to sit in chairs before the hearth and make idle conversation with Godfrey as they waited. Christopher thanked Godfrey for housing his men, and Godfrey insisted they had become a welcome addition to his troops. Godfrey's wife, Lady Alinor, served them ale herself, along with little cakes flavored with rosemary.

Before long the bath was ready. Dafydd followed Christopher up the stairs to the solar, and they found Alain waited for them there.

"Would you have me attend you?" he asked.

"Nay, we will attend ourselves," Christopher said.

Bowing his head, Alain left the room.

"You must needs bathe first this time, my king," Dafydd said.

"I would have you join me. The tub is large enough for us both. We have two days' journey ahead of us before we reach home and a proper bath." Christhoper smiled at Dafydd before turning to begin removing his clothes.

"Aye, 'tis true," Dafydd said, and he also began to disrobe.

Christopher could not contain his sigh of pleasure as he sank into the fragrant tub. The warmth melted away tension and eased muscles tired of sleeping on the floor. He watched through his eyelashes as Dafydd finished undressing and turned toward the tub. Scooting back and spreading his legs, Christopher gave Dafydd the room he needed to settle in front of him.

"Relax, cariad." He wrapped his arms around Dafydd's waist and bent forward to press a wet kiss upon his shoulder.

"'Tis nice, my king, to feel your body holding mine thus." He sighed in pleasure as well.

They sat this way for quite a while, with Christopher's arms and legs wrapped around Dafydd's body. When the water began to cool, Dafydd sat forward and reached for a cloth and a scoop of the clean-smelling soap. Behind him, Christopher reached for his own cloth and soap.

Washed and rinsed, Dafydd rose from the tub first. He took up a towel from the warming rack and handed it to Christopher before reaching for his own.

"Though we have privacy and a comfortable bed, I would wait until we reach the haven of your own bed at home," Christopher said once he had dried and set his towel aside.

"Aye, 'tis my wish as well," Dafydd said.

When Christopher and Dafydd descended the stairs a short time later, they found the hall below was already set for dinner, and their men mingled with the inhabitants of Sir Godfrey's keep. They were greeted with smiles all around, and a festive mood was felt by all.

Before they sought their seats, Christopher took time to speak with the captain of his guard. As he had expected, the men had been treated well. Christopher was anxious to leave early on the morrow. The distance from Sir Godfrey's keep to Lysnowydh was too great to cover in a single day, so it was agreed they would seek shelter in the Abbey of St. Michael.

Once all were seated, Christopher stood. "I would thank you for housing us within your borders, Sir Godfrey. Sir Dafydd and I have met with naught save good cheer whilst we have sojourned here. 'Tis proud you should be, as your people have shown discretion." He paused and took up his goblet. "Long will you and your people reside in my good graces."

As one, the people stood, and the room resounded with cries of "Hear!" Goblets and tankards were raised, and the meal began. Fish and new vegetables were followed by roasted beef and hearty bread. Dried apples soaked in wine and covered with clotted cream rounded out the meal, and 'twas several hours before all sat back, sated.

While the tables were cleared, Christopher sat before the hearth with Sir Godfrey and Dafydd. Their goblets were refilled, and a fire blazed before them. As Dafydd watched and listened, Sir Godfrey and Christopher recounted the many campaigns they had stood together. There was an easy camaraderie between them, and it allowed Dafydd to see Christopher in a different light. This added to the arsenal he had built of favorable things about the fierce king who loved him.

Eventually talk dwindled and Christopher rose from his seat. "We must needs make an early start on the morrow. Godfrey, I would seek our bed. Give my thanks again to your lady for allowing us your solar."

"No need for thanks, your majesty. We give it freely," Sir Godfrey said as he stood and bowed.

"'Tis well," Christopher said. He turned to watch Dafydd stand, and together they walked from the hearth toward the stairway. "I bid you good sleep."

"And to you," Godfrey called after them.

Above, in the solar, Christopher shed his clothes with Alain's help while Dafydd sat to remove his boots. Once Christopher was settled amongst the furs in the bed and Alain had departed, Dafydd stood and disrobed. He blew out the candles still burning on the hearth and went to join Christopher beneath the furs.

Twining their fingers together, they bent forward for a kiss, felt the promise that they held in their hearts, and they drifted to sleep.

Return

ALAIN came to wake them early the next morning. He helped Christopher dress while Dafydd dressed himself. Together they descended the stairs. There they broke their fast with Sir Godfrey and his men.

Once the meal was completed, they bid their hosts farewell with a promise to return during happier times in the summer, and then they joined the men in the misty bailey. All were mounted and ready to depart within a few minutes.

There was a chill in the air, and once clear of Sir Godfrey's lands, the men spread out, each lost in his own thoughts. Christopher rode behind Dafydd and to the side, so that he could watch him as they rode. He knew Dafydd's inner turmoil while the others who rode with them did not.

Toward the middle of the day, the sun burned through the clouds and warmed the air slightly. As they came upon a level part of the moor, Christopher called a halt that they might rest and have a small meal. The men ate hunks of bread, and Christopher and Dafydd augmented their meal with an apple that they shared between them.

There were still many miles to cover before they reached the Abbey of St. Michael, so they did not dally long, and when they remounted, they kept to the same formation, with Christopher again riding so that he could keep his gaze on Dafydd.

Christopher knew with shocking clarity all the turmoil Dafydd kept locked away inside. With the silence broken only by the sound of the horses' hooves on the rocks, Christopher's thoughts drifted to Dafydd's retelling of the torture he had suffered at Warin's hands, and his heart twisted within his chest. In that moment, everything snapped into place, and he understood why things could never be the way they had once been. Every hardship Dafydd had faced was a direct result of his being Christopher's mate and the light of his eye. Had they never met, Dafydd would have lived the balance of his life as woodsman or maybe as a healer. While Christopher knew beyond the shadow of doubt that Dafydd was content, there was a tie between his former life as king's marshal and the hardship he had suffered. Even though the memories had been expunged, the connection would remain. A strangled gasp issued forth, and Dafydd turned to meet Christopher's eye upon hearing the sound.

Although all the anguish had been again buried, Christopher knew it was still there. Dafydd smiled, and Christopher felt his heart untwist and melt as he returned the smile. He vowed silently that he would no longer push Dafydd to resume the responsibilities he once held. Breaking ranks, he rode closer and laid his hand upon Dafydd's for a bare moment, then spurred his horse forward.

The sun was just sinking below the horizon when they arrived at the gates of the abbey. Because Christopher was the king, his party was allowed entrance. Food was brought, and they passed a silent meal. After eating, the men went straight to the dormitory to sleep. Christopher murmured that he would like a moment of Dafydd's time, and together they walked out into the open courtyard, away from prying eyes.

"Are you well?" Christopher asked.

"Aye," Dafydd replied.

Christopher moved closer but still did not touch Dafydd, as he knew they were watched. "I love you, mayhap more now than ever before." He knew it was not the place to reveal the epiphany he had

had while they rode earlier that day, yet he hoped by saying this much, it would serve as a reminder that he needed to reveal all to Dafydd at some point in the future.

It was Dafydd's turn to shiver, and he bowed his head. "Aye, that same feeling is strong in me."

They separated then and went back inside. The king was granted a wall chamber, and even though the monks could not acknowledge the strange bond between Christopher and Dafydd, he was given a wall chamber as well. Both got into bed fully clothed and fell into a deep sleep. The day had been long, and the day that faced them would be equally so.

Early in the morning, a solitary rider departed and spurred toward the mighty keep at Lysnowydh. Christopher had been parted from his people for an extended period of time, and though he knew they were kept well in Sir Richard's hands, he knew also that they would be eager for his return.

The rest of the party left the abbey soon after, and again they rode in a column, well stretched out, each kept company by his own thoughts. At midday they once again stopped for a meager meal and were back in the saddle quickly for the final leg of their journey.

As the shadows grew long at the end of the day and landmarks were recognized, Christopher spurred closer to ride alongside Dafydd. "'Tis late," he said, "and when we return, I desire a meal and then to bed. Our bath will wait until the morrow. There is much to be done."

"Aye," Dafydd said. After a short silence, he added, "I offer my apologies to have kept you from your duties for this long."

"Nay, do not apologize. 'Tis behind us, and I would not spend overlong determining where fault lies, if indeed there is fault to be found. In matters of the heart, we learn together. In future we must needs both endeavor to share that which troubles us."

"You have my promise," Dafydd said.

As they were within the inner regions of their own kingdom, the riders continued as the sun set and darkness fell. The trip from Sir Godfrey's keep could easily take three days, but in their haste to return to the comfort of home, they had squeezed the journey to two days.

Once the keep came into view, they saw that torches lined the crenellations, and they heard the sound of the army amassed within the walls. The outer bailey was a chaos of soldiers and peasants alike, all raising a cheer to see their king and his woodsman safe returned.

The inner bailey was slightly more sedate, but as the horses clattered in, a loud howling started in the stables. Dafydd smiled as he slid from his horse and knelt in the dirt. In the early days of his union with Christopher, Patrick had gifted Dafydd with a puppy. As Patrick grew, so did the dog, and now Dewi nearly knocked Dafydd over with his greeting. For a moment Dafydd let the enormity of all that had transpired well up inside him. He buried his face in the scruff of fur at the dog's neck and wrapped strong arms around his body. Murmuring affections in Welsh, he took a private moment to count his blessings.

"You have been missed," Christopher said as he approached.

"Aye," Dafydd said, betraying his emotion as his voice cracked. "'Tis a reminder I shall not stray from home again." He stood and dusted himself off.

"Come," Christopher said. "I am told a meal awaits."

The weary men made their way up the outer steps and into the hall. The meal set out on tables close to the main hearth was a small one, but it was welcomed by all.

"I would meet with the council in the morning," Christopher said tiredly as Sir Walter approached. "There is much to discuss."

"As you wish, your majesty," Sir Walter said as he bowed. "I but sought to tell you that Sir Richard still resides in the keep, and he is eager to meet with you and the council on the morrow."

"'Tis well," Christopher said.

Their hunger sated, Christopher and Dafydd rose from the table and made their way upstairs. They parted at the landing, with Christopher going on to his chamber to be attended to by Alain, and Dafydd continuing into his own chamber to undress alone.

After climbing into bed under the warm furs, Dafydd felt tight muscles relax as he settled into the comfort of home and routine. A myriad of thoughts flickered through his mind as he gazed into the flames and waited for the telltale sounds of Christopher coming through the connecting chamber. His eyes heavy, he began to drift off, then was startled awake by the feel of the bed dipping and the warmth of the king pressed along his back. Even though he was nearly asleep, he reached for Christopher's hand and pulled it up against his chest.

"Sleep, cariad," Christopher murmured.

Twisting his body, Dafydd settled against Christopher with their foreheads pressed together. He rested his hand against the small of Christopher's back. "'Tis good to be home, anwylyd."

Pressing closer and brushing his lips against Dafydd's, Christopher whispered, "It is." And he knew then that all would be well.

Renewal

EARLY the next morning, Christopher stirred awake. Though there was much to be done and it was his wont to arise early without disturbing Dafydd's slumber, this day he took a moment to stretch out beside Dafydd and press his warmth along Dafydd's back. After a sleepy greeting, he said, "I would meet with the council this morning whilst you reacquaint yourself with your stillroom."

"Aye," Dafydd murmured, his voice hoarse with sleep yet. "And would you wish me to address the council as well?"

"Mayhap in the afternoon," Christopher said. "There will be no need for you to explain yourself. What is betwixt us, remains betwixt us."

"I know, and yet I wish to take responsibility for my actions," Dafydd said.

"I will not argue with you, yet you know there is no need to take responsibility for actions that were provoked by my own." Christopher eased closer for a kiss. He pulled back and rose from the bed. He turned to gaze down at Dafydd. "You are a strong man, Dafydd. Betimes you possess more strength than I am able to muster. Remain abed whilst I bathe, and then 'twill be your turn."

Mulling over Christopher's words, Dafydd admitted to himself that many times he did not feel he possessed strength at all. Even though he and Christopher had come to terms, he still hid the fear that, when presented with the opportunity, he would not have the strength necessary to follow through on his promises. Though the thoughts were weighty, he drowsed, snug in the warmth and comfort of his bed.

When he started awake, he realized that not much time had gone by, but enough that he knew Christopher was done with his bath. Indeed, when he entered the bathing chamber, he found it was empty. John had laid out fresh clothing but left Dafydd to bathe alone, as was his custom. Dafydd took the time to luxuriate and enjoy the soothing caress the warm water offered.

When he descended the stairs some time later, he found the keep settled into its normal daily routine. He took up a heel of bread, a slice of cheese, and a tankard of ale, and carried all to his stillroom. There he found all in readiness, the floor swept clean, a fire in the hearth, and his dog Dewi snoring in a corner. The peace that had descended over him while he bathed took firm root now as he began to reacquaint himself, as Christopher had suggested, with the dried herbs and mixtures.

Though he had longed to linger over his own bathing, Christopher had finished quickly that he might meet with the council. After breaking his fast, he had gone straight to the council chamber, and in the quarter of an hour he had to himself, he marshaled his thoughts.

There was no need for anyone in the kingdom to know what had transpired between him and Dafydd, unless Dafydd wished them to know. 'Twas Christopher's goal to smooth over his absence and advise his council of Dafydd's new functions within the kingdom. Then, if time permitted, he craved a private audience with Sir Richard. As much as Christopher had been away from his duties, he knew Richard had sacrificed his own duties that he might stay and see to the running of Lysnowydh in the absence of its leader.

The first to arrive in the chamber was the dour-faced Father Geoffrey. Since Dafydd had first taken up residence in the keep, Father Geoffrey had shown his distaste numerous times. In the main he found it difficult to hide the fact that he found Christopher's leanings unnatural, though his remarks always fell short of true censure. Although his greeting was warm, it was clear he was not pleased to hear Dafydd had returned.

Sir Walter arrived next, followed by Sir Henry and Sir Cuthbert. Their greetings were genuinely warm, as were their solicitations after Dafydd's health. Sir William and Sir Richard arrived last, and it was clear to Christopher that William had settled into his role as marshal: he carried himself as a leader.

Once all were seated, Christopher steepled his fingers together. "I would ask that you save your reports for a later time. There is much we need discuss this day."

"There is not much to report, your majesty," Sir Walter offered. "'Twas peaceful, in the main, whilst you were from home. Sir William drilled the troops in preparation for summer and warmer weather."

"'Tis well," Christopher said. He was silent for a moment and then took a deep breath. "Sir Dafydd has returned and is above in his chamber. Before long he will come below stairs to reacquaint himself with his stillroom."

Although he opened his mouth to speak, Father Geoffrey fell silent under the quelling look Christopher gave him, and the others held their peace.

"My word is law. Sir Dafydd will relinquish his duties as marshal, and give them over to Sir William permanently. In future, Dafydd will assume the role of healer for Lysnowydh. He will seek in the villages for those who will serve as his apprentices. Should the time arise that his strength is needed in battle, his shoulder will fit well with mine own. Beyond that, I am not inclined to speak further. What was is settled betwixt us; as such, you shall accept that 'tis done."

Before the others had a chance to form thoughts, Sir Richard spoke. "I speak for us all, your majesty, when I say we accept your word as law. There is no need for explanation."

"'Tis well," Christopher said. He tipped his head to the side as he watched the men he trusted so well. He knew they had questions, yet they were too well trained to ask. After a moment, he said, "'Tis also Dafydd's intention to retain his position with this council. He has offered to come before you this afternoon, if you feel 'tis necessary. Know this, however: he means to apologize for actions he had no choice but to take. I deem apology on his part is unnecessary."

Although he was usually silent on the rare occasions he was pressed to join the council, it was Sir Cuthbert who spoke first. "If you grant me the right to speak freely, your majesty," he said, pausing long enough to see Christopher's nod. "Mayhap I know Sir Dafydd's strength in battle more keenly than anyone else. 'Tis mine own humble opinion that he need not apologize to the likes of us. I judge not his decisions, and 'tis happy I am to see his return."

"Aye," Sir Walter chimed in. "I believe we all know Sir Dafydd in different ways, and speaking for myself, I have seen his intelligence and even manner. I too am glad he has returned, and require no apologies or explanations for his absence."

Agreement was murmured from Sir Henry and Sir William, and knowing he was outnumbered, Father Geoffrey nodded his assent.

"'Tis rare I speak of matters of the heart, yet in this I am greatly pleased. I would request that this day you return to your normal duties. Council will resume on the morrow." Christopher stood with the others and reached out to lay a hand on Sir Richard's arm. "Might I detain you for a word?"

"Aye, your majesty, you need not ask," Sir Richard said with a smile.

After pulling chairs from the council table and dragging them before the hearth, the two men sat side by side, their heads bent close together.

"In times such as these, I crave the counsel of my father, but as he is departed, that duty falls to you," Christopher said quietly.

"Aye, 'tis an honor I cherish, standing in the shoes of a dear friend," Richard said.

"You told me I must needs find the reasons that Dafydd fled on my own, in my own way. As I made my quest, the image of him formed in my mind." Christopher paused and then turned to meet Richard's steady gaze. "I found him near Godfrey's keep, at an inn by the sea. 'Tis my belief we have left whatever bitterness there was betwixt us in that far-off and wild place."

Richard remained silent, allowing Christopher to continue the story when he was ready.

"'Tis painful to speak of, and whilst I prodded him to rid himself of the demons he harbored, I find they now inhabit me. 'Tis a yoke which will bond us, each to the other," Christopher said, his voice rough with emotion.

Richard reached over and laid his hand upon Christopher's where it rested on the arm of the chair. "Such is the way, as it is for my lady and me: common joys and common sorrows, and they bind. By sharing his pain, you lessen it."

"Aye, 'tis truth," Christopher said. He closed his eyes for a moment, and when he spoke, his voice was low, barely heard. "I but knew that Warin was an evil man, with evil designs in his head and heart, but hearing the torture he meted out on one that I love, 'twas a difficult task."

"Do not torment yourself, Christopher," Richard said. "Dafydd would not want you to change who you are, a fierce warrior. I suspect at heart you do not want him to change who he is, a gentle soul. Mayhap in early times the knowledge is startling and hurtful, but 'tis my belief that as time passes, the pain eases."

Christopher slipped his hand from underneath Richard's and laid it atop the older man's. "I would that you speak with him. 'Tis strong in his soul that he feels he need apologize for his lack. I would not want him to do it before the whole council; he does not see that only weakens him. Yet I would feed his desire to empty some of the anguish he still holds within his heart."

"If he would speak, I would listen. I hold both of you as dear as I hold my own kin," Richard said fervently.

With a wan smile, Christopher withdrew his hand. "My thanks."

"As I have said, your gratitude is not needed," Richard said. "'Tis with pleasure I serve you."

"I believe you will find him ensconced in his stillroom," Christopher said.

"Then I shall find him and intrude upon his solitude," Richard replied.

DURING the winter months, Dafydd's supply of healing herbs had diminished. He looked forward to the coming spring and the time when he could renew and build his stores. With the apprentices Christopher had promised, Dafydd knew that his stock would not dwindle this way in the future.

At midday, Dafydd felt apprehensive about joining the rest of the keep for the meal, although he knew the longer he delayed, the more awkward he would feel. On this first day, he deemed he would stay out of sight. He set about brewing a calming tea, and with all his attention on the task, he was startled when Sir Richard entered the room.

"I have brought a trencher, that we might share the midday repast," Richard said by way of greeting.

"You but read my mind," Dafydd murmured as he pulled the small pan with the tea from the fire.

"Mayhap," Richard said as he set the plate on the table and indicated Dafydd should eat. "Or mayhap I understand that betimes solitude is fitting when one faces uncertainty."

Dafydd held the pan toward Richard, his eyebrow raised.

"Save the tea for yourself," Richard said kindly. "I have brought a tankard of ale."

They ate in silence for a time, until at last Dafydd took a healthy swallow of tea and perched on a tall stool. Finishing a last bite, Richard took up his tankard and found another stool.

"I would offer my ear, Dafydd, should you need," Richard said. "Not to betray confidences, but Christopher believes you feel need of justifying your flight."

Dafydd grunted and took another sip of his tea before answering. "When I sought refuge with you, I told you I had an unnamed fear. 'Twas my belief that if I faced it, I would conquer it. In that, I was only partly correct. Traveling such a long distance from my refuge did much to assuage the fear; spending time in quiet commune with Christopher finished the job."

"Methinks the fear will never truly be gone," Richard said, "and in truth I have no desire to hear that which engendered it in the first place." He was quiet for a moment and then continued in a quiet voice, "Those here in Lysnowydh keep need know nothing more than you have returned. They will benefit and be glad of your place here as healer. Though you wish to apologize, 'tis not necessary. Continue on as you were before, and over time things will come right once again."

Though tears blurred his vision for the barest moment, Dafydd displayed no other emotion to convey what the simple message meant. He waited a moment, then swallowed hard before he said, "My thanks."

28
A Test of Resolve

DAFYDD joined the keep in the lighter evening meal that night in the main hall. There were many hearty greetings, and Dafydd realized, as Sir Richard had counseled, that there was no need on his part to apologize or explain. Christopher's presence beside him was comforting nonetheless, and when the meal drew to a close, he caught Christopher's eye long enough to communicate not only his desire but his need. Bending closer, Christopher whispered in his ear to go above and wait, and that he would join Dafydd shortly.

A shiver of anticipation chased down Dafydd's spine as he mounted the stairs. The intimacy of home had been sorely missed.

As was their standard routine, John had already visited Dafydd's chamber. A fire blazed in the hearth, and a branch of candles stood lit on a low table by the bed. The furs were drawn back, and Dafydd's bed robe lay draped over the end of the bed.

Shedding his clothes before the warm fire, Dafydd felt himself fill with anticipation. He remained before the hearth, opting not to don the robe, and waited for Christopher to join him.

Before long, Christopher appeared through the adjoining door, and once he had shed his robe, he walked closer and pulled Dafydd into his strong arms. For the moment, they stood locked in one another's embrace, swaying before the blaze, breathing in each other's comforting scent.

Christopher reached up and gently cupped the side of Dafydd's face as he pulled back slightly. He traced Dafydd's lips with his thumb and then leaned in closer for a kiss. Dafydd tightened his arm firmly around Christopher's back and returned the kiss with all the fervor that was given.

"I must needs have you, cariad," Christopher gasped breathlessly when the kiss was broken.

"You always have me, beunydd." Dafydd's voice carried a moan of desire. He twined his fingers with Christopher's and led him backward toward the bed.

No further words were needed as they settled back amongst the furs. Christopher touched Dafydd's flesh with gentle fingers and kissed his fluttering eyelids. Dafydd clung to him, tasted Christopher's skin, and spread his legs to allow him to settle between them.

Neither wanted to break the bubble of longing that rose between them. They were content to take their time now they were home.

When their bodies joined, Dafydd arched up, wailing loudly at the sensation of pain tinged with passion. He gripped Christopher's shoulders tightly, and when the cry subsided, he pulled up to lay his cheek against Christopher's chest. He felt the wild beating of his heart and willed the world to stop for just that moment. Held against Christopher this way, he felt his cock throb between their bodies.

When at last Dafydd released his hold and settled back against the furs, he kept his eyes open as he watched Christopher above him. Even as he neared release, he did not close his eyes, and he saw in the depths of Christopher's eyes a deep, abiding love.

Christopher held back until he felt Dafydd's release, and only then did he close his eyes and give in. When the peak was passed, he spooned behind Dafydd's body, wrapped him tightly in his arms, and whispered, "I love you."

"'Rwy'n dy garu di," Dafydd murmured.

At last the chill in the room touched them, Christopher wrenched the furs over them, and they fell into a peaceful sleep.

In the morning, Christopher lingered long enough to kiss Dafydd awake and vow his love again.

"I would build the fire in you now, cariad," Christopher whispered, "that I might burn this night."

"And you shall," Dafydd said.

The day was given to the council. Dafydd joined them briefly in the morning and excused himself after the midday meal to return to his stillroom. Although Lysnowydh had remained at peace during the time that Christopher had been absent, there were still many things to discuss, chiefly the tributes owed and a schedule for collecting them once Beltane had passed.

"I shall delay my annual sojourn until midsummer," Christopher said. "'Tis my belief that Sir Dafydd will accompany me, and I would give him time to choose his apprentices first."

"Aye," Sir Walter said. "In truth 'twill be nice to have you both at home for a stretch."

Amid the murmurs of agreement, a clamor arose outside the chamber doors. Sir Walter rose and rounded the table just as someone began a thunderous pounding on the door. All were surprised to find one of the soldiers, called in from the yard, standing on the threshold.

"Begging pardon, my lord. Your majesty, there are riders from the outlying border near Tryger with news. 'Tis urgent, so they say." Other soldiers crowded behind the one who had knocked.

"Christ's blood," Christopher said as he rose from his chair. "What message do they bring?"

"Raiders, your majesty. They bring news of raiders," the soldier said.

As one, the rest of the council stood and trailed in Christopher's wake as he walked quickly into the hall. Two men, red-faced and dusty, stood just inside the hall, craning their necks anxiously for a glimpse of the king. The commotion had rousted Dafydd from his stillroom, and all converged in the center of the room.

"Beg pardon, your majesty," said the older of the two as he bowed his head. "We was taken by raiders this morn, near on an army, from over the border toward Tryger."

"Raiders?" said Christopher, bending his head closer to hear above the din that surrounded them. "What manner of raiders? Cattle?"

"Nay." The man raised his head in order to make eye contact with Christopher. "They was set on mischief, methinks. Set fire to our outbuildings, near run off with one o' the lasses had we not stumbled on them in surprise like."

Many thoughts whirled in Christopher's mind as he listened to the report. He recognized these men; they had a small holding granted to them by his father. It bordered Tryger yet fell outside the protection of Lysnowydh's lesser nobles. Although he knew not the reason for the invasion, he knew it needed to be dealt with swiftly.

"William," Christopher roared as he turned, nearly bumping into Dafydd, who stood close beside him. Sparing Dafydd one small look, Christopher turned to address his marshal. "We will mount a force, ride for Tryger this very day. I know not what deviltry this is, but it must needs be stopped."

"Aye, your majesty," William said with a curt bow, and he turned to gather Sir Cuthbert that they might mount up a party to ride forth.

"I would go with you," Dafydd said, his voice soft.

Christopher reached for Dafydd's hand and squeezed it tightly. "There is no need, cariad. Stay and ready your herbals lest we need care upon our return."

Dafydd squeezed Christopher's hand tightly when he made to pull away. "Nay, my king. I would ride with you."

Pausing and seeing the desperation in Dafydd's eyes, Christopher nodded once. He bent closer to speak softly for Dafydd's ear only. "I understand your intent, Dafydd, but know that I do not expect you to push yourself so soon."

One small crack in his voice betrayed the deep conviction Dafydd felt. "I know you do not expect it, yet I expect it of myself. If I mean to put weight behind the promises I gave you, I must needs do this. I am safe, as you have given your word, when I am beside you."

"'Tis well," Christopher said, and he turned quickly to hide the emotion that welled inside him. It had been his fervent desire that Dafydd would follow through. He had believed in his heart that he would, but seeing proof filled him with joy. Adrenaline surged at the prospect of dealing with the raiders and the knowledge that things would return to some semblance of normalcy.

❦ 29 ❦
No Small Fear

WITHIN a quarter of an hour, a troop was mounted and spurring away from the keep. Christopher rode at the head, alongside the two messengers. Sir William and Sir Cuthbert rode at the rear, keeping watchful eyes on those chosen to accompany them. Dafydd rode, head held high, hands gripping the reins tightly, in the center of the formation.

It would not take long to reach the site of the raid, and with the renewed fervor of the king and his consort, something told the men it would not go well for any who were caught.

A plume of black smoke, appearing as an angry gash against the blue sky, signaled the site of the raid. The king and his riders pulled abreast of one another on a hillock overlooking the once-peaceful valley. 'Twas clear to see the raiding force had come from a stand of trees and had indeed taken the small compound by surprise.

Christopher took the lead down the hillock and across the heather toward the cluster of buildings that made up the center of the small holding. Once the inhabitants saw it was their king who approached, they streamed from the main building, their voices a babble as the troop assembled and dismounted from their horses.

"Peace," Christopher said, his voice firm. He looked for the elder, the chief of this hamlet. "Detail the attack. Tell me how it occurred."

The elder's skin was dark and tough from hours spent in the sun farming and tending the small herd of cattle allotted to the holding. "'Twas dawn when we heard the noise, and by the time we heard it, 'twas too late. They fired the buttery and surprised young Guy as he was drawing water from the well." At this point he stepped forward and pulled a young girl closer, holding her protectively against himself. "My granddaughter Joan was just coming away from the buttery when the raiders approached. If not for young Guy, she would have been taken."

"Tell me what you saw," Christopher said to the young woman, his voice modulated and softer now.

Joan trembled against her grandfather's side, and her voice broke with emotion as she spoke. "They was wild like, and fierce. I saw three, mayhap four. They grabbed for me, tore my dress."

A muscle tensed in Christopher's jaw. "Can you tell me what they looked like?"

She buried her face against her grandfather's jerkin. "Dark," she mumbled. "Dark skin and hair."

"Welsh," Dafydd murmured.

Christopher turned to take in Dafydd's expression, yet found it unreadable.

"They are still about," Dafydd said, looking directly into Christopher's eyes. "They mean to see your reaction, and they expect you will retreat and muster an army. Once you are gone, they will return, and there will be no escape for any hostages they mean to gather."

"Are you certain?" Christopher asked.

"'Tis their manner, aye," Dafydd replied.

Christopher was silent for a moment; the war of emotions that cascaded through him was evident on his face. At last he murmured, "Shall we storm the wood, take them by surprise?"

"Nay, 'twill not be a surprise. They have situated themselves well that there can be no surprise attack." Dafydd fell silent for a moment and then said, "Would you hear my ideas?"

"Aye, of course," Christopher said.

Dafydd turned and spoke to the elder. "Might we take shelter inside your hall?"

"'Tis privacy you wish?" the elder asked.

"Illusion," Dafydd said. "Let us all step inside the hall."

Leaving the horses tethered to a low post, all of Christopher's men went inside the hall with the elder. They clustered around to hear Dafydd's plan.

"You must needs take the men with you, retreat back up yon hillock until you are out of sight. Wait for a time and then return quickly," Dafydd said.

Cocking his head to the side, Christopher said, "I? What of you?"

Squaring his shoulders, Dafydd said, "I will remain, along with one other. Take two members of this household with you that our horses do not remain behind. When the raiders return, we will take them by surprise. 'Tis my belief that you and the men will return in time to aid in their capture."

Christopher was silent for a time, and then he laid a hand on Dafydd's arm and drew him away. He spoke in a hushed voice, as there was no chance for privacy in this small hall. "'Tis not necessary, Dafydd, to take this risk. Your plan is sound, as I knew 'twould be, but let another remain in your stead."

"No other understands the intent of the Welsh the way I do," Dafydd said. "'Tis not folly that I offer myself this way. I know what I do, and I believe you will return ere the skirmish is fully joined."

"Then I shall leave William," Christopher said, "and I shall return as the wind."

"'Tis well," Dafydd said.

They rejoined the rest of the gathering, and Dafydd outlined the plan. "William and I will remain behind," he said to the elder. "Choose two of your number to don our cloaks and ride with the king back up the hill. You will then resume your normal routine. Once the raiders are lulled into the belief that the king has abandoned you, they will ride forth once again, unsuspecting that William and I will surge forth to meet them head to head."

Although he appeared uneasy with this plan, the elder agreed, and men were chosen to take Dafydd and William's place. The villeins stood in a cluster and watched Christopher's party ride off, then nervously turned to resume their normal routine. They had no choice but to trust the men left behind, and in truth all could see the strength and fervor Dafydd and William possessed, yet the surprise raid still left them fearful.

Dafydd stood just inside the doorway of the windowless hall, scanning the line of trees, and thus he saw the first rider issue forth. Although both men drew their swords, Dafydd held William back until more raiders rode out from the stand of trees. 'Twas his intention to draw them all out so there would be no chance for escape.

"Now," Dafydd growled through gritted teeth, and he and William ran from the hall, swords held high.

As he had expected, the element of surprise was great. Allowing William to circle behind the small force, Dafydd went straight for the one he deemed was the leader.

"Hold," Dafydd roared as the man wheeled in surprise. "Dismount lest I cut your horse from under you. Stand and face me, or be labeled coward."

"You are but two men," the leader shouted. He laughed harshly. "You are easily overcome."

With a feral grin, Dafydd moved closer. "You seek to overcome the king's marshal. You will find 'tis not an easy task."

Snarling, the leader slid from his horse's back, and with sword drawn, he advanced on Dafydd. In his peripheral vision, Dafydd saw two other raiders slide from their horses and advance on William. Keeping his sights firmly on the leader, Dafydd rushed forward, and they were joined in battle.

Both Dafydd and William were well-trained swordsmen, and though the raiders were fierce, in truth they were no match for the combined forces of marshal and former marshal. Dafydd and William gravitated toward each other, and Dafydd took up a position at William's back. They worked together to hold their attackers at bay. When Dafydd shouted curses in Welsh, the men were startled, and soon looks of desperation began to cover the raiders' faces.

As they had planned, Christopher and the rest of the men streamed down into the hamlet and easily surrounded the band of Welshmen. Remaining at the center, back to back, Dafydd and William watched with grim satisfaction as each raider was captured in turn.

All eight men were seized and herded as cattle toward the large tree in the center of the holding. While his men dipped their heads, the leader stood with head held high, displaying all the pride of his race. He snarled at Dafydd and ground out in Welsh that he was nothing but a traitor.

Stepping closer and swelling with the rage and adrenaline that still coursed through him, Dafydd spoke in his native tongue. "Diawl, you have no grounds to hurl curses upon mine head. 'Tis you who is coward, mounting a sneak attack." He reached out and wrapped his fist in the smaller man's shirt, gripped tightly, and forced him to his knees. "Though I be Welsh, I stand firm with King Christopher of Lysnowydh. Seek to harm any that reside under his protection, and face his wrath. Seek to harm him, and face mine." Dafydd released his hold, turned, and strode back to join the men, leaving the raiders to hear their fate.

Christopher stepped forward to take Dafydd's place. He looked upon the group of men with disdain. The pride he felt in Dafydd, the love that bubbled inside him, these emotions he kept locked deeply inside.

"Hear this," Christopher roared, and even though the raiders did not cower before the king's might, they listened as their fate was announced. "For unprovoked acts of violence against this peaceful hamlet, all shall hang."

There would be no pleading for mercy, but it did not stop them from struggling against those who held them.

The king's men accepted dippers of water and hunks of bread from the grateful villeins. While the ropes were readied, Christopher watched Dafydd from the corner of his eye. A slight trembling of his hands was the only telltale sign that the skirmish had had a profound effect on him. In truth, Christopher felt a like tremor inside, yet he strove to squash it, as he would not show weakness before his men.

As the sun sank low in the sky, the raiders met their fate, and when 'twas done, the king's party began the journey back to Lysnowydh keep.

Peace Reigns

IT WAS late when the party returned home. Although the meal was ended for the night, Christopher requested a small tray be sent to Dafydd's room. He stopped long enough to recount the events of the afternoon to Sir Walter while watching Dafydd climb the stairs out of the corner of his eye. After promising to give a more detailed report the following day, Christopher turned to wearily climb the stairs himself, pausing on the landing long enough to dismiss Alain for the rest of the night.

When he entered Dafydd's chamber, he found the requested meal on a table in the corner. Dafydd had removed his gauntlets and cloak, and he stood motionless before the hearth, gazing into the flames. Christopher removed his own gauntlets and cloak and moved to stand beside Dafydd, keeping the silence between them for the moment. After a while, he reached over and took Dafydd's hand.

"How do you fare?" he asked softly.

"Well," Dafydd said.

"Would you speak of it?" Christopher asked.

"Nay," Dafydd replied.

Christopher squeezed Dafydd's hand gently. "Then I will not push you. Come, sit and sup." He released Dafydd's hand and turned to pull the chairs away from the table.

Dafydd sat and took up his goblet first, draining full half before he set it aside. He picked at the capon breast before finally murmuring, "E'en though I felt no fear, just as you said, 'tis well to have given the reins of power over to William."

"Dafydd," Christopher said as he pushed the plate of food aside, "here in your chamber we are not king and consort, we are lovers, friends, confidants. Here is a safe haven where we might speak freely with one another, mayhap say things we would not say otherwise, and certainly never admit outside this small circle betwixt us."

Dafydd nodded and remained silent, waiting for Christopher to continue.

"I have never doubted your strength, just as I have never doubted mine own. But here, in this safe haven, I will admit to you that I felt fear today, riding away and leaving you in harm's way." He held up his hand to stave off comment from Dafydd. "It made me see things in a different light. Though I know your strength, and I know you have proved yourself in battle, a sliver of fear remained in my heart, more so than I have ever felt."

"My king," Dafydd said, and he sat forward and reached for Christopher's hand. "In the moment, I felt no fear. I focused on what needed to be done, and 'twas no different from when I went to deal with Sir Edward's treachery. 'Twas after that the fear came forth."

"'Tis natural," Christopher said. After a brief silence, he continued in a soft voice, "As we returned from Godfrey's keep, I acknowledged in my heart that you would never resume the yoke of marshal, and I came to accept that." He squeezed Dafydd's hand to hold him off from speaking. "I knew 'twas not cowardice on your part. I saw clearly all the many reasons why your time as marshal was completed. Today, the reasons were clear when I saw that you still possess the strength, both of body and of mind, to deal with matters such as this." After another brief pause, Christopher took a deep breath. "'Tis well, Dafydd."

The only sign of the tremendous emotion that filled him was a welling of tears in Dafydd's eyes, and he squeezed Christopher's hand. They sat that way, joined hand to hand, until at last Dafydd said, "I would to bed. I have no appetite for food this night."

With a sultry smile, Christopher stood and said, "Yet you have an appetite for aught else?"

Stepping closer and hovering his lips over Christopher's, Dafydd murmured, "To be held by you, to drift to sleep feeling safe inside your love."

"'Tis well," Christopher replied.

Together they shed their clothes, and as Dafydd pulled the furs aside, Christopher blew out the candles. Once they were wrapped beneath the covers, Christopher pressed his lips against the back of Dafydd's neck. "Sleep well, cariad, wrapped in my love."

"Beunydd," Dafydd said, and he pulled Christopher's hand up and clutched it against his chest.

WITHIN a week, Sir Richard returned to his keep, and life within the mighty keep of Lysnowydh settled into its accustomed routine. It lacked only a few weeks until Beltane, and the castle folk buzzed with the knowledge that the day held a double blessing.

As the weather warmed, Sir William and Sir Cuthbert began to drill the troops in the outer bailey. New squires had been sent, and as was custom, their initiation fell to Sir Cuthbert and his captains. At the same time, Sir William re-formed regiments with the seasoned knights, and all worked in the accustomed manner.

Christopher split his time, spending mornings with the council and afternoons drilling with the troops. Sir Arnald, a landless knight who had worked his way up through Christopher's army and had proven himself worthy, was elevated to the council. During summer months when Sir William and Sir Cuthbert spent all their time with the troops, Christopher needed knights to participate in the council, giving the soldiers' perspective on doings within the realm.

Dafydd flourished in his new role as healer for the keep. Several apprentices were chosen from the village; most possessed a natural ability with herbals. Alain's wife, Alyce, was given charge of the infirmary, and the stillroom was Dafydd's domain. As the weather warmed, Dafydd took his apprentices into the forests surrounding the keep, looking for the plants he would need. As always, Dafydd craved the peacefulness of the woods.

The castle servants set themselves to a frenzy of cleaning, as was their wont at this time of year. Old rushes were raked from the floors and replaced with fresh rushes sweetened with heather. Walls were scrubbed of winter's grime. Even the hearth in the main hall was scrubbed clean.

One afternoon, as Dafydd worked in his stillroom, setting herbs upon the drying racks, he looked up to find that Matilda, the castle seamstress, had joined him. He smiled and came forward to greet her. "What brings you out of your sewing chamber?"

"You, Sir Dafydd," she said with a small curtsey. "'Tis nearly three years since I worked my fingers to the bone preparing a wardrobe for your handfasting to our King, and two years since I had the honor of watching our heir born. 'Tis with pride I have served our king lo these many years."

"'Tis well," Dafydd said.

She set a cloth-wrapped bundle on the table. "I admire you, Sir Dafydd, and I seek to honor you with this small token. 'Tis given from my heart, indeed from the hearts of all who serve in this keep. In early days there were those who resented your coming. In current times there are none who resent it. You have well and truly become cherished by all." She paused. "Mayhap I seek above my station in speaking such, but I have ne'er been one for caution."

Dafydd smiled. "Aye, Matilda, this I know." He pulled the bundle closer and carefully removed the cloth covering. Inside was a beautifully wrought carpet depicting a lion sleeping in a forest and a falcon perched on a tree overhead, keeping watch. Dafydd drew in his breath and touched the carpet reverently. "'Twill be a fine addition to King Christopher's chamber," he said.

"Nay," Matilda countered, and she boldly reached up to touch the carpet, her fingers close beside Dafydd's. "'Tis for your chamber, Sir Dafydd, to adorn your hearth. You deserve such warmth for your feet. 'Tis my gift to you for Beltane."

"I am touched," Dafydd said as he looked up and met her gaze. "My heartfelt thanks."

"'Tis naught," she said, and she straightened up. "I bid you a good afternoon."

"A good afternoon to you, as well," Dafydd said, and he rewrapped the carpet that he might carry it up to his chamber later.

THE following week, Patrick and Marged arrived from Strasnedh with Anwyll. A joyous celebration ensued as all welcomed the king's heir. Anwyll stood the inspection for a time, and then he cried and clung to his mam. Marged accommodated by taking him off and leaving him in the care of Anne before returning to partake of the evening meal.

"It hardly seems possible that it has been two years since we welcomed Anwyll," Christopher said that night as he shared the dais with Patrick and Marged. As always, Dafydd sat on his left side in the seat of honor. The position next to him that had long been Marged's when she resided in the keep was now given over to Sir William.

"He grows each day. He is already saying words," Marged said with pride.

"Aye," Patrick added. "He rode with me as we came here today, and already he seems at home on horseback."

"'Tis well," Christopher said.

"Beltane comes in four days," Patrick said as he sliced off a section of rare beef and presented it to Marged on the tip of his knife. "'Tis proud we are to be included in your celebrations here, your majesty."

"Our celebrations will be quite different this year," Christopher said. "In truth, that is the primary reason I have requested you come."

"Different? Might you tell us how, your majesty?" Marged asked.

"I but asked you both to come that Anwyll be here in my stead this year. Dafydd and I will attend the bonfire, as is custom, but we will not be present in the keep during the main festivities the following day." He scooped up some of the rich gravy in the bottom of his trencher with a hunk of bread. "I will but keep a promise I made to Dafydd."

Warm color covered Dafydd's features. He had all but forgotten the promise Christopher had made him when they were tucked away at the inn. Although they had taken time for themselves during last year's Beltane, they had still been tied to the festivities in the keep. For two years they had not been allowed proper time to celebrate the anniversary of their handfasting. Yet it did not trouble Dafydd overmuch, as he knew that Christopher's life was taken over more with kingly duties and less with the duties of mate.

"'Tis a promise I relish, my king," Dafydd murmured for Christopher's ears alone.

"Aye, cariad, as do I," Christopher said, and he laid his hand on Dafydd's knee below the table.

"'Tis an honor, your majesty, to preside with your son over the festivities here," Patrick said.

"One richly deserved," Christopher avowed.

31
Deep Bonds

'TWAS rare for Dafydd to wake before Christopher in the morning, and on the infrequent occasions he did, he took a moment to catalogue his thoughts, fearing that something was amiss. Christopher was beside him, his breathing indicating he was still deep in sleep. All around him, the quiet of the early morning exuded calm, but deep inside he felt something was wrong.

At last he rose from the bed slowly, so as not to disturb Christopher's slumber. In the darkened room he pulled on chausses and a fur-lined bed robe, which he belted tightly at his waist. As Dafydd stepped into soft felt indoor shoes, Christopher turned over in his sleep but did not wake.

Dafydd felt his way down the stairs without a candle and came out into the shadowy hall. There were still a few hours until dawn would light the sky, and none were about. He stood still, listening for a moment, until he heard a telltale shuffle, and he walked further into the room to find that Marged sat before the main hearth, Anwyll on her lap.

As he neared her, Dafydd cleared his throat so he would not take her by surprise. When she heard the sound, she turned, her hand gently cradling the child's back. "Sir Dafydd," she said softly, "'tis early."

"Aye," he said as he sat in a chair beside her. "Too early for you to be stirring about."

She smiled and patted Anwyll's back. "He sleeps early and wakes early. I think mayhap he has a molar pushing through."

Dafydd reached over, and without hesitation, Marged handed her son over. Finding himself jostled from the warmth of his mam, Anwyll opened his mouth to cry, but the cry caught in his throat as he made eye contact with Dafydd. He settled and gazed up into Dafydd's eyes as though he were mesmerized.

"Always, Sir Dafydd, you have a calming effect on him," Marged murmured.

"Ah, beraidd," Dafydd said, falling back easily into the pet name he had once used for her, "how soon you forget that when 'tis just us two, there is no need for formality." He hoisted Anwyll up against his shoulder and rubbed a gentle circle into his back. "'Tis early for molars."

"Aye," Marged said as she raised a hand and rubbed her eyes tiredly. "And yet the young master is early at everything. His first milk teeth came before he was three months old." She smiled wanly. "He is like his father, impatient for things to happen."

Dafydd turned and pressed a small kiss on Anwyll's ear and murmured softly, "Do not be so eager for things, bachgen. Everything has a time and a place." He turned to look at Marged. "Go back to your bed, beraidd. I will make a balm for his gums and hold him for a bit. You are tired, and you need your rest."

"Nay, Dafydd, I could not trouble you. I am used to early morns," she said.

"I insist," Dafydd said. "'Tis well I have time with him." He stood, still holding the now drowsing boy in his arms.

"I will send Anne to retrieve him in an hour's time," Marged said as she also stood. "If you wish to spend time with him, 'tis better served to spend it in daylight hours, when it does not deprive you of your sleep."

Dafydd smiled. "If I worried for my sleep, I would not have ventured below stairs nor made the offer. Now go, seek sleep, and worry no more for me or your son."

After dipping a small curtsey, Marged turned and headed out of the hall toward the sleeping chambers. Dafydd patted Anwyll's back and turned to walk toward his stillroom. As he walked, he murmured into the boy's ear softly.

As was his wont, Dewi slept in the corner of the stillroom. When Dafydd entered, Dewi raised his head and wagged his tail, pleased to see his master so early. When Dafydd bypassed him and headed straight for the table in the center of the room, Dewi levered himself up to follow and stood sniffing at Anwyll's foot after Dafydd perched him on the table.

Dafydd lit a candle and then rinsed his hands in a basin. Then he turned to look at Anwyll. The child was a melding of Christopher's elegant features and Marged's sturdy Welsh build. His hair was a sandy blond, his eyes deep brown. He looked at Dafydd steadily.

"Open your mouth, bachgen," Dafydd said, "that I might see this magical tooth that comes too soon."

Obediently Anwyll opened his mouth, and Dafydd moved the candle closer to peer inside. Indeed, he found a reddish bump in the back of his mouth, and he straightened up and set the candle aside. "'Tis truth, you have a tooth that is eager to come. 'Tis painful."

Anwyll nodded and put his finger back in his mouth.

"Cloves will be good for the pain, and a wee bit of chamomile," Dafydd said with a wink. "'Twill help you fall back to sleep."

Anwyll chewed on his finger and watched as Dafydd worked. Before long, Dafydd had ground the cloves and dried chamomile and added a bit of honey to make a paste. Anwyll obediently opened his mouth again when Dafydd put a bit of the paste on his finger and held it toward him.

Once the balm was soothed over Anwyll's gum, Dafydd picked him up, blew out the candle, and headed back to the hall. Dewi followed and settled at their feet. Embers smoldered in the hearth, but Dafydd was loath to set Anwyll in the chair unattended so that he might add a log and set the fire blazing. Instead, he drew the chair closer and settled Anwyll that they might both look into the embers.

"One day, this shall be your home, young Anwyll," Dafydd said quietly. "You shall rule, mayhap with an even hand, just like your father. You shall be fierce as a lion and gentle as a lamb, both are needed to make a fair ruler."

Snuggling up against Dafydd, Anwyll listened as Dafydd continued to talk. He spoke of the future and of the past. He spoke of Lysnowydh's history and of the many battles Christopher had won. Soon, Dafydd realized that Anwyll slept, and he fell silent.

Dafydd turned his head slightly when he heard a shoft shuffling step behind him, but not far enough to see who approached. "Seek your bed, Anne. The young master sleeps."

A firm hand was laid on his shoulder, and Dafydd looked up into Christopher's eyes.

"You are abroad early, cariad," Christopher said as he squatted down beside the chair.

"I woke and felt aught was amiss. When I came below stairs, I found Marged, wakeful with Anwyll's teething pains. I but offered to take him, that she might sleep," Dafydd said.

Christopher smiled and cupped the back of Anwyll's head. "You have given him quite the history," he murmured.

"'Tis proud I am of Lysnowydh and its ruler," Dafydd said.

"Aye, I knew that already e'en before I heard the last part of your words to our sleeping beauty here," Christopher said. He stood and then sat in the chair beside Dafydd. "'Tis early, yet soon the servants will be about, preparing for the day. Let us sit awhile, until Anne comes forth."

They sat in companionable silence, and as the servants began to stir, Anne came to fetch Anwyll. Although he woke, he did not fuss as Dafydd handed him over. Dafydd murmured to Anne that if Anwyll's pain returned, he would make more of the balm. She curtseyed her thanks and bore Anwyll off toward his sleeping chamber.

"You have missed quite of bit of your sleep, cariad," Christopher said to Dafydd when Anne was gone.

"Aye, and yet I shall make it up this night."

"Go and change. Come back that we might break our fast together," Christopher urged. "There are things that must needs be settled ere Beltane a few days hence."

ANWYLL made a lively addition to the proceedings over the next few days. He and Dewi became inseparable, and Patrick avowed it was fate, since he was the one who had gifted Dafydd with the dog three years earlier at Beltane. The molar seemed to subside, as if it had been testing the gum and decided to stay put a while longer. Anwyll had no more issues with the pain.

In the few days remaining until Beltane, the castle was a frenzy of activity. Agnes ruled in the kitchens, preparing for the feast that the keep and village would share, as well as for the private feast Christopher meant to share with Dafydd. Out of doors, Sir Cuthbert oversaw the laying of the bonfire, while Sir Walter organized an inventory of the cattle.

At the center of all the activity, Christopher was a pillar of serenity. 'Twas his wont to be petulant and easily angered when this much activity swirled around him, but he seemed to draw on some inner peace. None save Dafydd knew the source of Christopher's calm.

"I think mayhap I have gone soft," Christopher murmured one night as they lay abed, still tingling in the aftermath of their love play.

"Nay, my king, you are not soft," Dafydd said. He spooned behind Christopher, his hand possessively on Christopher's belly, holding their bodies close together.

"Things do not trouble me as they once did," Christopher said. "Where once I was quick to anger, now I am not. I know not the reason, lest it is I have gone soft."

"The fierceness is still inside you, Christopher. 'Twill never leave. When the time comes and there is something that truly angers, it will roar out like a lion." Dafydd pressed a kiss against Christopher's shoulder.

"Then what is the reason that I do not roar at all who burden me with petty worries?"

"'Tis that your worry abates and love fills the spaces," Dafydd murmured.

There was silence for a time, and then Christopher said softly, "As I have told you oft times, you are a poet, cariad."

"Aye, you have told me, and mayhap 'tis true," Dafydd said. "Yet I know that your love has filled in empty spaces all through mine own heart."

"Ah, then 'tis your love that crowds out my anger and worry," Christopher said.

"Aye."

❦ 32 ❦
Beltane Eve

THE day before Beltane dawned clear, and young men and women from the keep issued forth in abundance to hunt down hawthorn branches to adorn both the interior of the hall and all the outer spaces in the bailey. The keep was a whirl of activity. Tables were set in the outer bailey for the feast, and Matilda and her helpers adorned each one with an embroidered cloth. Sir Cuthbert and his squires were everywhere, ensuring the bonfire was laid and helping with all the final touches.

Having stirred early, as was his custom, Christopher found he was more underfoot than a help, as none would ask for his assistance and all were clumsy-fingered when he offered it anyway. At last he took himself to his council chamber, where he spent the morning alone.

After he arose and dressed, Dafydd deemed it unnecessary to venture below stairs. Although he knew he could lend a hand to the proceedings, he very much craved the solitude of his private stillroom. The room that adjoined his sleeping chamber had long been his haven; it was here he brewed his own personal stock of herbals, and it was always neat and tidy.

After breaking his fast with the bread and ale John had left for him, Dafydd entered his stillroom. On a shelf just inside the door sat a wooden box in a little niche. He took the box to the table and opened it reverently. Inside was his copy of the vows Christopher had recited to him on that very day three years ago.

They had known, even then, that their union would never be truly blessed by the holy church. As had become clear during Christopher's recent trip to London, it was likely not even viewed as official. They had been given false hope with the written document King Henry had bestowed upon them. As Dafydd lifted the parchment from the box, he considered that, in the end, it did not matter. He loved Christopher, maybe more now than he ever had, and it was not important to him to have official leave to marry. The words written on the parchment were what was important, as were his memories of that balmy day.

Because they had only been given leave to handfast, Christopher had determined he and Dafydd would ride to the beach on the day before Beltane. There, with only the gulls and the wild waves as witness, they recited actual wedding vows, vows that bound them together in their own hearts. The beach held a magic, as it was on the day of their first visit there that Dafydd's love had crystallized. On that day he had realized beyond a shadow of a doubt that the love Christopher professed so readily was echoed in his own heart. It was fitting that they should solemnize their union upon that beach, even if it meant naught to any save themselves.

As he unfolded the parchment, he closed his eyes and built the scene in his head. The wind had whipped around them; the sand had been soft below their feet. Christopher's hand had been warm as he held Dafydd's and led him to the outcropping of rocks. He did not need to read the words on the parchment, as they were etched upon his memory.

I take thee, Dafydd, to be my wedded mate, in sickness and health, for richer or poorer, through all the days of my life 'til death depart us. I promise to honor and respect you, to listen as you speak. I promise to hold you and cherish you, forsaking all others.

Dafydd's lips moved as he recited the words silently, felt all the familiar emotions well through his body, and even felt the weight of Christopher's fingers on his brow as he laid the circlet crown upon his head.

"I give you this pledge and with this token claim you for mine."

Startled from his reverie, Dafydd opened his eyes, and as if the strength of the memory had pulled him, he found that Christopher stood just inside the doorway.

"Might I join you?" Christopher asked.

"Of course, my king," Dafydd said as he stirred from the stool and dragged another over that Christopher could sit beside him. When they were settled again, Dafydd said, "You but read my mind."

"Nay," Christopher said as he reached for Dafydd's hand. "These thoughts were in mine own heart. I but came above stairs knowing you were in solitude here." He raised Dafydd's hand and pressed his lips against the back of it. "Betimes our thoughts travel the same path, and 'tis not a reading of minds, 'tis a bonding of our souls." He dropped Dafydd's hand, reached inside his tunic, and pulled out a folded parchment.

Without unfolding the document, Dafydd knew it was the words he had written for Christopher. Though he had spoken them in Welsh, he had written them in English that Christopher might know the depth of his emotion. Whispering, he spoke the words in English: "I, Dafydd, take you, Christopher, as my husband, in sickness and health, for richer or poorer, as long as we both shall live. Receive this ring as a token of my love and faithfulness. I worship you with my body and share all my goods with you."

"Cariad," Christopher said, and his voice broke with the emotion that welled inside.

As one, they rose from their stools, and Christopher pulled Dafydd into the circle of his arms. For a time they stood taking strength from one another, and then Christopher eased back, tipped his head, and found Dafydd's lips. Though it was a chaste kiss, each felt the passion inside the other, and when it eased, they resumed their seats on the stools.

"On the first Beltane after our handfasting, we renewed these vows, reflected on the fact that we knew not how our lives were to change in the months ahead of us," Christopher said. "Little did we know that though we lived through hard times, 'twould be so difficult to lay those hard times to rest." He held up his hand as Dafydd opened his mouth. "Hold, cariad, I must needs say this. Aye, we would but sweep it all aside, and yet I would ensure we are on even footing."

To cover the silence that fell then, Dafydd picked up the parchment and tucked it back inside its box. He kept his head down and waited for Christopher to continue.

"Mayhap on that day three years ago I should have added that I promised to protect you, not just to love, cherish, and honor you. And mayhap two years ago, when we acknowledged that our bond was stronger than we realized, I should have taken the time to ask after matters of the heart instead of feeling false confidence that all was well betwixt us." He paused and took a deep breath. "Ours is a forever bond, Dafydd. Our hearts are joined one to the other, as was vowed by Father Geoffrey. I believe in mine own heart that the events of a month past overcame any lingering hurt that was buried, I would but ensure 'tis so."

Christopher turned on his stool and faced Dafydd. "I would you look at me, Dafydd."

Though soft color bloomed across his cheeks, Dafydd turned and met Christopher's steady gaze.

"In future, I give you my bond to cherish you, and protect you, and love you without boundaries. This is my solemn vow." Christopher's voice was firm as he said the words.

"Your majesty," Dafydd said, and he held up his hand to stave off Christopher's protestation at the title. "Nay, you must needs let me speak. You are king, and as such, your first bond is to protect your kingdom. Mine heart swells to bursting at your promise to protect me before all others, yet know that I hold no anger that you chose to protect your own heir before me. 'Twas your future, and deep within me I knew you would not leave me behind." Dafydd's voice broke with his passion. "I knew you would not forsake me."

Dafydd reached across the table and took Christopher's hand. "I accept your bond now and give you mine own in return. On this day, three years removed from our handfasting, I vow we leave what is in the past, in the past and retain only the ashes of memories as proof positive that our love will not break."

"Aye," Christopher said, and he squeezed Dafydd's hand tightly.

Dafydd bent forward, touched his forehead to Christopher's, and then, after releasing his hand, he stood and reached for a small dish on the shelf above the table. Into the shallow dish he piled the stems of dried angelica. As he picked them up one by one and pulled the dried leaves off, he said, "Angelica is oft used in Beltane rituals. 'Tis said to ward off evil." When he was done, he swept the leaves into a square of muslin and tied the bundle, then put the stems back in the bowl. He took a brand, lit it in the small hearth that warmed from the corner of the room, and touched it to the pile of twigs until they caught fire. "Close your eyes, my king. Breathe in."

The aroma was not unpleasant, and in truth Christopher did feel peace settling through his soul. The stems did not burn long, and when they were done burning, Dafydd said, "Come, I will draw your bath. Soak with the herbs that evil might be kept at bay, at least until Beltane next."

"I give you a condition," Christopher said as he rose from the stool. "You must needs bathe as well, as I would do all within my power to keep evil from you, cariad."

With a small smile, Dafydd took Christopher's hand. "Then we shall bathe together."

Together they walked through Dafydd's room and into the bathing chamber. Whilst below in the keep, the flurry of activity continued, above in their private bathing chamber, king and woodsman soaked in an herb-filled tub. There was deep longing in each, yet they vowed to keep chaste until the morrow when they went off for their private sojourn.

Once the water cooled, they rose from the tub and dried, leaving each other as they went to dress in clothing appropriate for the evening meal and the bonfire afterward, vowing to meet on the landing after dressing.

When they ventured below stairs later, hand in hand and radiating peace, they found that the whirlwind of activity had eased and the hall was awash with flowers and smiling faces. The dais was bedecked, and Marged stood holding a smiling Anwyll, Patrick by her side. As though all could sense the new peace that radiated between king and consort, an unrehearsed cheer echoed through the hall.

Christopher smiled his thanks and gestured that all should take seats. The main feast was set for the morrow, yet all ate and drank well that night. When the meal was concluded, Christopher led the masses to the outer bailey and through to where the bonfire awaited.

"This night we celebrate the second year of my son Anwyll's life," Christopher said, and he was forced to pause whilst the gathered masses cheered.

Startled from a doze, Anwyll fretted at first, and would have gone off into a full-blown bout of crying had Dafydd not taken him from his mother's arms. As always, Dafydd had a calming effect on the boy, and he settled.

"Though it be still off in the future, one day young Anwyll will rule in my stead," Christopher continued. "Though he resides now in Strasnedh, in the protection of his mother and Sir Patrick, once he is of age, he will live here in Lysnowydh, serve as squire, and eventually become knight. This Beltane, let him preside over your festivities on the morrow. Honor him as you honor me."

A roar rose from the crowd, and at that moment Christopher signaled that the bonfire be lit. An ale cask was breached and tankards were passed all around just as Dafydd handed Anwyll back to Marged.

The revelry would last through the night, but soon after the fire was lit, Christopher bid farewell to his people, dismissed Alain and John for the night, and departed back for the castle with Dafydd close upon his heels.

"Desire," he whispered to Dafydd as they mounted the stairs. "I would hone mine this night that I might greet you will all my strength on the morrow."

"'Tis well," Dafydd replied, and he bent forward for the whisper of a kiss. "Until the morrow."

Turning from each other, each entered his own chamber.

33
A Heart Given

DAFYDD woke early the next morning and found that John had already visited his room. The fire burned in his hearth and clothing was laid out over a chair. Instead of breaking his fast with bread and ale in his chamber, as was his wont, Dafydd put aside his drowsy dreaming that he might rise and dress.

The clothing was not as opulent as it had been on the morning three years in the past, but it was befitting of marking the reverence of the day. A snowy white linen shirt, deep-brown leather jerkin, supple doeskin chausses, and sword belt completed the outfit. He sat to tie leather boots on his feet. When he stood, he reached for the shell that still took a place of honor on his mantel, and after rubbing his thumb over it lovingly, he tucked it inside his pouch. All that remained was his crimson cloak and his circlet crown.

As he expected, Christopher waited for him on the landing, and the sight of him took Dafydd's breath away, as it always did. The blue velvet of Christopher's jerkin accented his eyes, and the regal crown added to all that had attracted Dafydd to him in the first place. For a moment his knees were weak.

When Dafydd stepped forward, Christopher held up his hand and bid him stay back a moment. As Dafydd watched, Christopher opened his pouch and pulled out the shell Dafydd had given him on the beach below the inn.

"I know you but carry your own shell as talisman, just as you did on that day three years in the past. This shell is part of our reconciliation, and in my mind 'tis proof that we shall never be torn asunder again." Christopher's voice was soft.

"My king," Dafydd murmured.

"Come, cariad," Christopher said, "The faster we dispatch our duties this morn, the faster we retreat."

Dafydd stepped forward and tucked his hand into Christopher's, and together they descended the stairs.

Only a few stragglers remained in the hall, as most had made their way out to the bonfire. Those who did remain were bleary-eyed, yet all smiles for their king and his consort. It was still dark as they made their way down the stairs, through the bailey, and out through the open front gate.

The mighty bonfire had burned down to glowing embers, and those not fortunate enough to be close to its warmth passed wineskins between themselves. As Christopher and Dafydd approached, the crowd parted and let them through, and they arrived just as the sky began to light with dawn. Raucousness that had prevailed through the night died down as all watched the sun crest over the horizon.

Christopher and Dafydd were silent with their own thoughts as their faces were bathed in the light of the new day. Each reminisced on the past, yet each looked to the future.

Once the sun was higher, the cattle were brought forth to plod slowly alongside the fire before being driven out to spring pastures. Most of the assembled mass turned to trudge up the hill to the chapel before the last of the herd left the pen. A few foolhardy young shepherds leaped over the bed of glowing coals.

Father Geoffrey's service was short, touching only on the hope for a bountiful year and the blessing of the king's heir surviving his first years of life. Nothing was mentioned of the king's happiness with his mate, and yet Christopher did not expect that would be included in the priest's sermon. There was still an uneasy acceptance on the part of the priest, and Christopher recognized that it would always be so. When the service was finished, Christopher reached for Dafydd's arm and held him back to his seat in the family pew.

When they were alone, he turned and spoke quietly. "As always, Dafydd, I cherish this day as it united our souls."

"Aye, as do I," Dafydd said.

"Though 'twill not be mentioned by Father Geoffrey, know that 'tis always within my heart on this day," Christopher said.

"As it is in mine," Dafydd said, and he turned and bent closer for a small kiss.

"I burn," Christopher murmured against Dafydd's mouth.

"Then we must needs break our fast that we might venture forth and quench the flames," Dafydd said.

"Wicked," Christopher said as he stood.

"'Tis as you expect," Dafydd said with a wink.

Tables for the feast were set up inside the walls of the inner bailey. A few of these were laden with bread and ale, and those who had not found a quiet corner to sleep off the effects of too much revelry the night before milled about, eating and preparing for the day of games.

Although he was anxious to be off, Christopher led Dafydd to where Patrick stood with Marged and Anwyll.

"Greetings," Christopher called as they approached. "Dafydd and I would break our fast with you ere we depart."

"'Tis well," Marged said, and she struggled to hold the wiggling Anwyll. "He yearns for you, Dafydd," she said with a small laugh.

Smiling, Dafydd reached out and took Anwyll from her arms, bending closer to whisper for his ears alone, "Careful, bachgen, lest your mam become jealous."

Anwyll gurgled and settled happily in Dafydd's arms. Marged's eyes welled with tears of pride to see the two together, and she was far from being jealous. She knew it had been Christopher's intent to find a Welsh woman to bear his child, and the effect was stunning. Although Anwyll was clearly Christopher's son, he did bear some features that resembled Dafydd's dark looks.

Once the hasty meal was finished, Christopher gave his final blessing to Patrick and Marged, and he said farewell to the members of his council. Only Sir Walter knew where they were off to on their sojourn, and his lips were sealed.

Before the first dance around the maypole began, Christopher and Dafydd were mounted and cantering down the road that led away from Lysnowydh. When they turned left instead of right, Dafydd closed the distance between them and rode abreast with Christopher.

"I had thought you meant to pass the day in your hunting lodge," Dafydd said.

Christopher cast an innocent look Dafydd's way. "Did I say that?"

"Aye, when we tarried by the sea."

"I have no doubt you can guess where I mean to take you," Christopher said. "In truth, though I do remember that I said the lodge, I also remember where you wished to spend the day. I have chosen to honor your desires, as they feed mine own."

It was true that once they turned, Dafydd knew Christopher meant to pass their sojourn in his old cottage. So much history of their love was centered there. It was where they first met, it was where Christopher had announced his intention to handfast, and it was also where they were the day Anwyll decided to enter the world.

As they continued the ride in silence, Dafydd contemplated that there were a few places in the kingdom that would forever hold a special place in their lives. This cottage was but one, as was the beach, the keep, and even the hunting lodge. Even though both had vowed to keep the past in the past, he also acknowledged that the inn below Sir Godfrey's keep would forever be added to this list of special places within the kingdom.

Golden sunlight dappled through the trees, looking almost green through the new growth. They stabled their horses before venturing into the small cottage. All was in readiness. A fire burned in the hearth, and their feast was laid out on the table, covered in snowy-white cloths. Another chair had been brought from the keep, and Dafydd's crude horn bowls had been replaced by Christopher's fine wooden trenchers. Flowers bedecked every flat surface, and the bed had been replaced by one finely crafted in the keep.

Once inside, Christopher turned and said to Dafydd, "Do you hunger, cariad?"

"Aye," Dafydd said as he came up to stand behind Christopher and wrap his arms around him. "Yet 'tis not food for which I hunger, 'tis you."

"'Tis as I expected," Christopher said, and he clamped his hands on Dafydd's arms, holding them tightly. "Yet I would spend this time in your arms yet a while."

Dafydd nuzzled against Christopher's ear and murmured, "'Tis well."

There was a peacefulness here in the woods that each felt. 'Twas quiet away from the hustle and bustle and demands on their time. Each revisited their first meeting, and each remembered it differently: Christopher remembered being cold and weary, seeking shelter from the storm. Dafydd remembered the deep honor he felt when the king chose to shelter with him.

At last, Christopher turned, twined his arms up around Dafydd's neck, and whispered, "I would give you that which you desire most this day, my sweet Dafydd."

Dafydd bent his head, took Christopher's lips in a full kiss, and then whispered, "I would see you first, anwylyd."

With a small shiver, Christopher stepped backward and began to disrobe. Hasty fingers were tangled over knots in drawstrings until Dafydd lent a hand. When Christopher was naked, he turned and helped Dafydd undress. Soon, they stood face to face across the furs strewn before the hearth.

"Name your desire, cariad," Christopher said, "that I might gift you with it this day."

"I desire what I have always wanted, my king," Dafydd said, and he lifted one hand, palm up. "I yearn your heart and all the love inside of it."

Christopher made a sound that was a cross between a gasp and a moan. He lifted his hand, pressed it against his chest, and then held it out toward Dafydd. "You have always had my heart, Dafydd, since first I laid mine eyes upon you."

Stepping forward, Dafydd took Christopher's hand in both of his and raised it to his lips. He kept his eyes locked on Christopher's as he kissed his hand and then turned it to place against his own chest. "I love you, so very much."

Once Dafydd released his hand, Christopher caressed gently over his chest, down his side, around to cup his hip and draw him close. He stood for a moment, breathing in Dafydd's scent before he whispered, "And I love you, equally as much."

The thin hold they had over their passions snapped in that moment, and Christopher sank to his knees, pulling Dafydd down with him. "This day is ours, with no interruption. I must needs have you here before the fire, and later in yon bed."

Worming his hand between their bodies, Dafydd caught both their cocks together and stroked upward, feeling his shudder echoed in Christopher. "As you burn, I also burn."

Christopher angled his head down to watch as Dafydd stroked them both, and whispered raggedly, "Now, cariad."

Without releasing his hold on Christopher's shaft, Dafydd lay down on his back against the furs. He arched up for one searing kiss, then let go and reached down to pull his leg up against his body. With eyes hooded with desire, he watched Christopher turn for the pot of cream set on the hearth.

When he turned back, the fire lent a glow to Christopher's body, lit his hair like a halo or the lion's mane of Dafydd's imagination. He paused a moment to gaze down on Dafydd's body, so ready to receive him. Reaching down with slickened fingers, he touched Dafydd gently, felt his muscles soften and give way.

"Mmm… cariad… you feel good," Christopher murmured as he slid his fingers free and reached for more of the cream.

"'Tis your touch," Dafydd said, a hitch in his voice. "I would feel you inside me."

"Shh," Christopher crooned as he slid his fingers inside again and leaned forward to press a kiss upon Dafydd's knee. "Soon."

It was this subtle balance of control that pulled Dafydd in. In truth, with Christopher's patience and fierce love, he felt back on even footing. It was within his power to shift the balance of control, but now he allowed it and tingled in anticipation. He pushed up against Christopher's questing fingers and did not hold back his moan of desire.

"Cariad." The endearment was a mere whisper on Christopher's lips, and once again he withdrew his fingers. This time he slathered the cream upon his length. "Look at me."

It was not a struggle to keep his eyes open, and he groaned as Christopher began to slide inside. "Eiddoch."

"Aye, you are mine," Christopher groaned, and he bent closer, folding Dafydd in half as he eased close for a kiss. "Beunydd."

"Always," Dafydd murmured.

Burning desire overcame them, and Christopher straightened up and began to move within Dafydd, gently at first, and then hard enough to slide Dafydd's back along the floor. As they gave themselves over to the total abandon, no further words were needed between them. All was raw emotion.

Dafydd broke first. His neck arched up off the floor, the cry of release caught in his throat. Feeling the warmth that bathed his belly, Christopher closed his eyes, slammed in one last time, and held as his body shuddered with release. Blindly, he reached for Dafydd's hands and twined their fingers together.

"Fy llew," Dafydd whispered. "My lion."

Still buried deep inside Dafydd's passage, Christopher raised his head, met Dafydd's gaze. "You are as fierce as a lion yourself, cariad."

Dafydd smiled and rolled up to claim a deep kiss.

"We must needs to bed," Christopher said breathlessly when the kiss broke. "These old bones cannot take much of this hard floor."

"Aye," Dafydd murmured. "I would not be parted from your warmth just yet."

As they stood and walked the few steps to the bed, Christopher said, "I am sure we will but build our appetite through the afternoon. I would not offend Agnes by not eating her feast."

"We shall need sustenance, my king; I mean to worship you with my body many times." Dafydd waited while Christopher settled in the bed, and then he climbed in beside him. It was warmer in the cottage than it was in the castle, and there was no need for covers.

"Likewise," Christopher said, and he turned on his side to look upon Dafydd. They had spoken on the past so often, and there was no need to bring the shadow between them here, but he was pleased with Dafydd's response, even more convinced that the corner had been turned and the evil specter of Warin would not trouble them again. "There is aught I want from you too. 'Tis not to be one-sided."

Turning, Dafydd met Christopher's gaze. "What do you desire?"

"I desire your heart as well," Christopher said simply.

Moving closer, Dafydd dropped his arm over Christopher's hip and said, "'Tis easy, my king. Just as you claim I have always had your heart, you also have always had mine."

Christopher shifted forward and pressed his lips against Dafydd's chest, felt the steady pulse of his heartbeat below the flesh. "'Tis well," he murmured.

Sated after their self-enforced abstinence, king and woodsman drifted into a light doze. They would wake later to taste each other once again, and when the shadows grew long, they would share the ample feast.

As Beltane was the start of the summer months, once again it was a beginning to the love they shared.

Epilogue
Two Hearts Joined

BEES moved lazily in the garden, from blossoms of yarrow to the delicate flowers of feverfew. There was a pleasant scent here as the summer sun baked the ground. Dafydd paused to run the back of his hand across his brow. He sat back on his heels, pleased with the variety of plants that grew here. True, the weeding could be left to his apprentices, but he derived great pleasure from tending the plot himself.

Dafydd heard Christopher's voice, raised with command, as he drilled the squires on the other side of the wall that separated the garden from the bailey. A hazy memory flitted across his mind, of a time he had delivered a load of wood for the king's kitchen and found Christopher at work with his troops.

Dafydd gathered his tools, stood and walked through the neat rows of the garden, stopping long enough to pluck a rose from the bush by the door. He continued into his stillroom, where he stowed his garden tools and expertly trimmed the rose before setting it in a crockery dish. It was late afternoon, and the apprentices had finished their work for the day.

With one final pass through the room to ensure all was set to rights, Dafydd took the small dish and ventured forth into the hall. The tables were already in place for the main meal, and he set the dish before Christopher's place at the dais.

As the servants began to issue forth from the kitchen with food, Christopher walked through the main entrance, and the troops streamed in after him. His face lit when he saw Dafydd already standing by his chair, and he strode across the room. He swept Dafydd into his arms and kissed him deeply.

"'Tis glad I am to see you," Christopher said as he stepped back.

"'Tis glad you are each day when you see me," Dafydd teased, and he pulled Christopher's chair back from the table.

"Aye, 'tis truth," Christopher said. "Yet this day I am doubly glad."

Arching a brow, Dafydd took his own seat. "And why, pray tell?"

"Mayhap 'tis a secret," Christopher said, and he reached forward for the rose, lifted it to his nose, and breathed in the sweet scent before setting it back in its dish.

Chuckling, Dafydd turned to wash his hands in the basin held out to them by the page boy. "I believe I can guess."

After washing his hands, Christopher waggled a finger in Dafydd's direction. "I think you cannot."

Bending closer, Dafydd whispered against Christopher's ear, "In two days' time 'twill be Lammas-tide, and a feast day. You made a promise once, that each year on Lammas we would repeat the part of Beltane that we both enjoyed the most. You must remember that."

"Curses," Christopher said with mock anger. "Am I to have no secrets from you?"

"Mayhap," Dafydd said, and he served the rarest slice of beef onto Christopher's trencher and took another slice for himself. "'Tis just that in truth, I had the equal joy at seeing you this day, because in my heart I yearned for Lammas as well."

"Wicked," Christopher said as he took up his knife.

"Aye, but 'tis my belief you enjoy my wickedness," Dafydd said.

"Christ's blood," Christopher exploded. "Mayhap I must needs take you to my hunting lodge in two days' time, see about getting some of this wickedness out of your body."

Dafydd speared a piece of beef serenely and murmured, "I suppose you could try."

Christopher threw back his head and laughed long and hard. The others in the hall smiled at the sound, knowing full well that love had not abated between the king and his consort, and likely never would. All had experienced balmy days of peace during this summer season, and all expected the peace would reign for many years to come.

How the story started

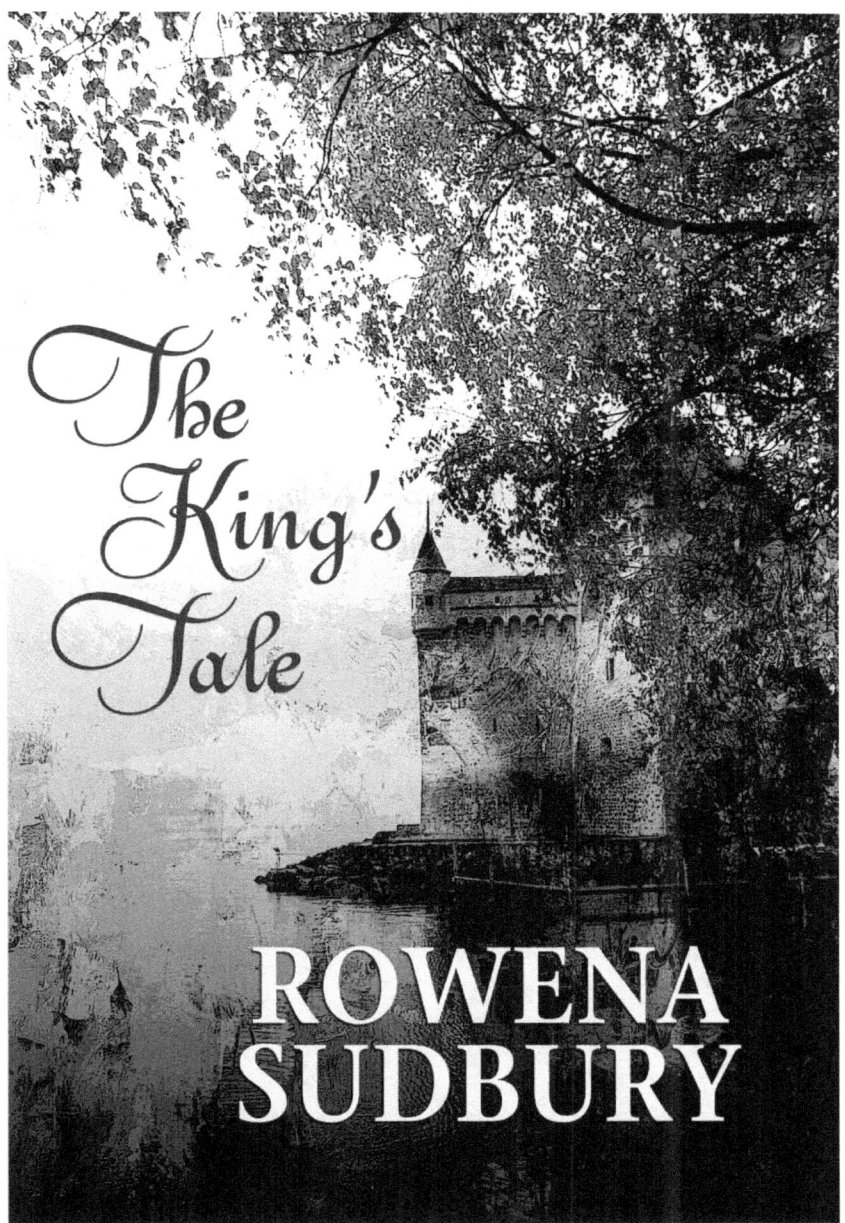

The King's Tale

ROWENA SUDBURY

ROWENA SUDBURY lives in southern California with her husband, son, and their wonderful rescue dog. Her love of reading was born in the fifth grade, and she began writing soon after that. Writing has always been her passion and escape from the real world.

Rowena finds herself thinking through the minds of her characters quite often, to the point that she always has to carry a small journal with her so she can capture their thoughts and weave them into stories when she gets home.

Visit Rowena's blog at http://rowenasudbury.livejournal.com/ and e-mail her at rowenasudbury@gmail.com.

Also from ROWENA SUDBURY